Night Watch

Night Watch

Susan Zettell

Signature
EDITIONS

Cover design by Terry Gallagher/Doowah Design.
Printed and bound in Canada by AGMV Marquis Imprimeur Inc.

Acknowledgements
Parts of this book have been previously published: "Carmen Waits" and "Facts About Niagara" in *Quintet* (BuschekBooks, 1998), "River Pictures" in *Pottersfield Portfolio*, "Remembering Her Young" in *Room of One's Own*, "Night Watch" in *The Fiddlehead*, "Nimbostratus" in *The New Quarterly*.

The author would like to thank the Regional Municipality of Ottawa-Carleton, the Ontario Arts Council, and The Canada Council for the Arts for financial assistance.

Thanks to Laura McLauchlan, to Rita Donovan and John Buschek, to Susan Brown, The Ottawa Writing Group: Gabriella Goliger, Debra Martin, Nadine McInnis, Sandra Nicholls, Kim Reynolds, Barbara Sibbald and Vivian Tors-Grabstas and to my Freefall Writing Group: Beth Ferguson, Jane Keeler, Helen Levine and Faith Schneider.

As always, thank you to my friends and family. A special thanks to Nancy Zettell for breakfasts and companionship, and to Karen Haughian for her kindness and guidance.

We acknowledge the support of The Canada Council for the Arts and the Manitoba Arts Council for our publishing program.

Canadian Cataloguing in Publication Data

Zettell, Susan, 1951–
    Night watch

ISBN 0-921833-74-1

    I. Title.

PS8599.E88N54   C813'.54   C00-901206-0
PR9199.3.Z49N54 2000

Signature Editions, P.O. Box 206, RPO Corydon
Winnipeg, Manitoba, R3M 3S7

for Andy

Night Watch

Remembering Her Young

This curve in the highway where willow branches dance over the stony banks of the Grand River is as familiar to Bernice as the contours of her Aunt Miriam's body. Bernice pulls over to watch the water flow. She hasn't been home in two years, so a little more time won't matter. She closes her eyes and the river's path is projected like a film onto her eyelids. She lifts her hand from the steering wheel to trace lines—Miriam's hair, neck, back, legs—on the soft fabric of the car seat. She reaches for the open letter there beside her:

> I am so old and tired that I find it difficult to write or talk! Please remember me young.
> Miriam

Remembering Miriam, it's smells that come first, a fruity-sweet mix of oranges and sunshine. All year round Miriam hangs her clothes to dry outdoors. Even when her breath reeks of liquor her clothes hold the scent of wind, mown grass, frosty earth, musty leaves.

That long-ago day in February, after her daddy left and her mommy spent her time crying and forgetting Bernice was there, Miriam came to take Bernice away. Miriam smelled of snow and wet wool. She put her hand on Bernice's shoulder, pulled her close to her long legs. Bernice's cheek rubbed on the rough green pants. Bernice was seven.

"She'll be fine, Janet. I give you my word. Robert and I will take good care of her," Bernice's Aunt Miriam said.

Bernice remembers that leaving day, those smells. And the sight of her mother's back as she turned to go into the house without saying goodbye.

"This is too much for us," Bernice heard her Uncle Robert say from the kitchen after she had gone to bed on the roll-out sofa.

"Shut your mouth," Miriam hissed at him.

Bernice decided then and there, lying between sheets that felt cold and sad, that she didn't need a family. Didn't want one. But she'd live with Miriam and Robert until it was time to go away.

That's the way it was. Though once or twice Bernice was tempted to relent, she didn't. What's done is done. Miriam taught her that.

"Your daddy was a no-good and my daddy was worse," Miriam said, though when she looked Bernice straight in the eye she hesitated. "Well maybe not worse, but what's done is done. Finis.

"My daddy—your grandpa—was a mean cop and a drunk. I remember times when he begged my mummy to drink with him. 'Just one, Mary,' he'd say. He knew she had a bottle hidden somewhere in the cellar. Down on his knees crying into her skirt. 'Have one with me now, Mary.'

"After she let him suffer awhile she'd pour one for him and one for herself. His went down his gullet; hers went into a pan on the chair beside her. It was their game. She saved those pan drinks for when he came begging."

Then Miriam sighed and wrapped her arms around Bernice, pulled her close and hugged her, kissed her on each eyelid. Bernice let her do this.

"You don't have to tell me anything," she said into Bernice's hair.

That summer, Bernice's mother ran away to the States with some no-good trash trumpet player. That's what Miriam told her. Bernice didn't cry.

"Shameful, that's what it is," Bernice overheard Miriam say to Robert. "We're all she's got."

When Bernice left for university, Miriam gave her a bust of Shakespeare that she'd ordered with her Gold Star stamps. And a photograph album with pictures right from when Bernice was a baby. Robert gave her a brand new one hundred dollar bill and vouchers for long distance calls.

"In case you get lonely for us," he told her.

Bernice spent the money. The telephone vouchers still sit in a drawer in her kitchen.

¤

Bernice's Aunt Miriam is five feet, eleven inches tall; her hair is as wiry and coarse as rusted steel wool and exactly that colour. Sometimes Miriam hennas it, turning it into a flaming orange mass.

"The way it used to be," Miriam tells Bernice.

Then it shines and flashes in the light like electrified copper wire. Her breasts are like two hard cantaloupes that stand out just above her high waist. She has no bum to speak of, and her legs seem to stretch on forever, starting with long slim feet, toenails painted crimson every summer, trim ankles, perfect calves, thighs as tight and shapely as a model's.

"Robert took one look at these legs and he turned to mush," Miriam told Bernice. Bernice admitted to liking these stories: how Robert courted Miriam.

"Hubba, hubba," Robert winked at Bernice. "Your aunt's legs go from the ground to heaven with a stop for honey halfway there."

"Hush, you," Miriam told him, but she grinned and grinned.

Before she was married, Miriam worked as a waitress behind Woolworths lunch counter. Robert came every day on his break to drink the bottomless cup of coffee. Sometimes he ordered a tin roof sundae, sometimes chicken salad on brown, toasted.

"Every time Miriam leaned into the freezer to get ice-cream I grew an extra leg. I thought I'd have a heart attack right there."

All the time Bernice lived with Miriam and Robert, whenever they wanted to be especially tender or make up after a fight, one or the other would make a pot of coffee, get ingredients for tin roof sundaes—vanilla ice-cream, chocolate sauce, salted Spanish peanuts—or make chicken salad sandwiches. They would sit at the table, eat, talk with Bernice, include her in the glow of their love. They'd laugh even when things weren't really funny, their voices low and throaty. Then Robert and Miriam would leave Bernice, go to bed, close the door behind them, their hushed whispers mixed with sighs and laughter long after their light went out.

Sometimes Miriam went on a tear.

"Nobody's perfect. I can't help it, Bernice. It's in my blood like poison. I take that first drink, I want more and more and more," Miriam told her.

Once, when Miriam was on a binge, Robert woke Bernice up at midnight and they painted the steps—front and back—with bright red oil paint. A thick lazy coat of it. They painted themselves in, Miriam out.

"This'll do it," he told Bernice who sat on the porch floor holding the paint can. "I know Miriam. Even drunk, she'd never walk on wet paint."

Robert was right. They found Miriam lying on the morning newspaper, her coat tucked under her chin. As they stood over her, she pulled one arm from under the coat, raised her middle finger. Her finger was painted red.

Another time when Miriam hadn't been home for three days, Robert drove his car through the emergency room doors at Memorial Hospital. He tried to make a left turn down the hallway but the car wedged tight. The police had to break the front windshield to get him out. A sergeant told Bernice and a hungover Miriam that Robert wouldn't be charged, but the damage must be paid for. He told them that Robert had shouted,

"Help me, I'm bleeding inside. She's broken my heart and it's bleeding right here inside me."

"He's so dramatic," Miriam told Bernice after they had left Robert sedated and resting in the hospital. But Bernice could tell her aunt was shaken. "What if he'd died?" Miriam whispered in the taxi going home. Then she recovered. "I hate cops. I bet that sergeant beats his wife," she said loudly.

When they got home Miriam told Bernice to strip the beds and get all the towels and clothes. They were going to do laundry. They washed and hung out everything made of cloth. It took the whole three days Robert was held for observation. Their hands were raw and wrinkled. The house smelled of soap and wind-blown summer air.

"For a clean start when Robert gets home," Miriam said. "And I'm going on a diet. Get rid of this." She grabbed a handful of the solid flesh on her hips.

Miriam bought an exercise video. As the clothes dried on the line, she watched it.

"I'll never be able to do that," Miriam groaned.

The instructor was on her knees lifting her leg like a dog peeing, first one side, then the other.

"Never in a million years."

When Robert came home he seemed fine.

"Fit as a friggin' fiddle," he said. "God, it smells good in here."

After that, the tables turned. If Miriam started to drink, Robert left home for as long as it took for her to come to her senses. Sometimes he stayed at the Flying Dutchman Hotel out on the old highway.

"I checked," Miriam told Bernice.

Once he moved in with a redhead who looked so much like Miriam when she was younger, it almost made Bernice cry. Soon after that Bernice went away to university.

It is dark when Bernice arrives at her aunt's house.

"Robert's been gone for two weeks and I'm not even drinking," Miriam tells her.

Bernice watches as Miriam makes coffee. Her face is haggard, grey shows at the roots of her brassy hair. Her body is bloated.

Miriam catches Bernice watching, turns her back and says, "I know what you see. I'm in here somewhere, Bernice." She faces Bernice, pokes at her fleshy belly, her arms, her cheeks. "I can feel the young, thin me inside all this."

Miriam sighs, then looks up at the ceiling and laughs.

"See that hole? A stovepipe used to go through there. One time my friend came to stay. She had two fat babies too fast. After we put the babies to bed, we had a beer."

As Miriam talks her body relaxes; her voice gets dreamy.

"We kept hearing this sound like squirrels in the wall or something. We ignored it, but it kept up. Then I looked up and saw these fat baby legs going back and forth in the air. Right out of the stovepipe hole, waving like crazy."

"I guess the baby got up and walked right into that hole. We laughed all the way upstairs. When we saw that baby's head sticking up out of the floor, his eyes as big as saucers, we had to sit down, we were laughing so hard. Funny thing was he didn't cry."

Miriam laughs, face glowing, lines gentled out. She brushes tears from her eyes.

"He was none the worse for wear." Miriam looks directly at Bernice.

"I had a baby once. I was sixteen. My daddy locked me in my room, only my mummy was allowed to visit me. They took my baby away before I got to see it. I heard it cry, though. I saw it was a girl when I signed the papers."

Bernice would like to shift her eyes from Miriam's but she can't.

"My daddy wouldn't let me go back to school, so I got a job at Woolworths and met Robert. I never told anybody about my baby, not even Robert. And nobody ever asked, not my friends, nobody. It just didn't happen, I guess."

"I thought I never wanted a child after that. Then you came along. I couldn't say no. You and Robert are the best things that ever happened to me."

Bernice has been motionless. Now she gets up. She pours more coffee because she must do something ordinary or she will cry. She hasn't cried in this house since her first night on the roll-out bed. There is no sound but their breathing. Then the sound of Robert's car.

Miriam rushes to the door and locks it. She turns out the lights. She sits at the table, her back straight, both feet flat on the floor, her hands folded around her coffee cup. She stares at some point on the wall. She doesn't blink.

"Let me in," Robert yells as he bangs on the door. He goes to the front door and tries it, all the time yelling, "I know you're in there, Miriam. I know it!" He throws stones at the windows and the walls. He sings "Knees Up, Mother Brown" as loudly as he can.

"Aunt Miriam, someone called the police," Bernice tells her aunt.

Blue lights swirl through the kitchen, flash across Miriam's still face.

"Don't touch me," Robert screams.

"I'll have to arrest you. Is that what you want?" someone screams back at him.

Miriam rises from the table.

"I hate cops," she says, as if this explains everything, as if this is all Bernice ever has to know about her.

She opens the door. She stands behind it. Light pours in from the street lamps, from the headlights of the police car, from its whirling warning flashers. She stays behind the door until Robert walks in.

"I'm going," Bernice says and walks out. She doesn't think she can bear the intimacy of Miriam and Robert's reconciliation. How happy they would be to include her.

Bernice gets into her car. She opens the window. She hears a train and the rhythmic boom of heavy equipment from the factories nearby, sounds she'd always heard from her bedroom window all summer long.

Bernice notices laundry on the line and gets out of the car. She goes to the washline, watches the ghostly shapes float back and forth on the breeze. She begins to take the laundry down, folds each piece carefully into the basket Miriam has left beside the pole: white sheets luminous in the dark. Pale, empty clothes hopeful with the promise of vitality and drama. She sniffs the night-freshened airiness of each article; she fingers flaws, small tears, the gauziness of fabric thinned and fragile, one movement away from destruction.

Bernice decides once and for all. She will stay at The Flying Dutchman Hotel. She will order a scotch and she will let the whiskey help her to remember all that needs remembering about her mother and father, about Robert, about herself. And about Miriam when she was young. Tomorrow, when she is ready, she will return to her home. To Miriam and Robert. And while she visits she will begin to accept the embrace, the imperfect caress, of this mystery she calls family.

River Pictures

My father is dying in Cape Breton. I should be there with him. Instead, I am with my sons, Neil and Thomas, on a small beach along the Saco River in New Hampshire. The day is summer perfect, the sky empty and as smooth as a starched blue shirt. I swear I can see each individual tree on the mountainsides. The Presidential Range, the map tells me. Pretty. Not threatening like the mountains out west. I went to Banff once, just after my divorce. The Rockies made me think my hurt and despair were small things, that there was nothing I could do that was as important or as frightening as those mountains.

These mountains that rise out of the fields around the Saco aren't a worry. It's certain they've seen accidents. And death. But on this day the light from the sky slices into the water and reveals everything: minnows flashing like knife blades angled to catch the sun, black-green mossy rocks, slimy, rotting fallen limbs from the birch and pine trees which lean over the bank.

And there's sand. Fine, sifted and pale, inviting me to walk into the water slowly, down onto its soothing smoothness. It is beige in the shallows, darkens to an earthy brown, becomes greenish-looking where the water deepens and the sand gives way to rocks and muck and moss.

In Cape Breton the Barachois moves faster and there are rocks and boulders everywhere. It doesn't invite a picnic as you pass by. It is the kind of river you have to live beside for a lifetime to learn where to swim, or picnic, or take a fish. The water is tinged red and foams along the edges after a good rain. And although you can see the rocks clearly enough in the shallows, its deep bottom is a mystery.

When I was young my brother's friend Donnie drowned
in the Barachois. He was walking along the edge on the rocks and
he slipped in and disappeared. The river carried away the slight
ripples he made. My brothers, Davie and Sandy, and I dove and
dove. It took twenty minutes to find Donnie, suspended near
the bottom, his body shifting slightly in the current like a
tendril of moss on a rock. His eyes were open and seemed
almost alert.

He was dead when we pulled him out, but we worked on
him, Davie on his chest, Sandy and I taking turns on his mouth,
Donnie's head tilted back, his nostrils pinched shut—one, two,
three, BLOW, one, two, three, BLOW—until the ambulance
came. When I think of Donnie now, I think of how fat solidifies
in the body after death as the body's temperature lowers. And
how water, especially cold water, is a good preservative, even
though it causes bloat. These are not happy thoughts, or even
relevant, but they persist nonetheless.

My father never entered the water, not even on the hottest
days. He spent his time on the shore or riverbank trying not to
get sunburned and counting heads. Shouting orders: "That's too
deep, come back here where it's shallow." "Stop that stupidity,
someone will get hurt." "Ten more minutes and we're leaving."
"It's time to go. Now! I said now!"

What he really wanted was to get home and have another
beer, the three he'd brought in the car gone. Or something
stronger. He only drank the beer because my mother made him,
because if he was going to drive the car anyway, which he was,
it was safer, she said. She never said out loud what it was safer
than and she never let him take more than three.

When my mother was dying, when her skin stretched over
the lumps of her bones like raw, rolled-thin dough over apples
in a pie, my father began to drink more heavily and took a series
of lovers. Some of the women were friends of the family. He
brought them to the house while my mother was in hospital
receiving treatment. That summer my father sent Davie, Sandy,
and me to camp on the mainland. Every two weeks, after each

scheduled session ended, he came to pick us up, sometimes with one of his friends. We begged him to let us stay.

During my mother's remission, my parents took a trip to Florida. Their friend Glenda Harrington went along. To help out, my father said. All of the photographs from that trip were of Glenda. My mother wrote in her album: Glenda by the St Johns River. Glenda by the North New River Canal on the way to South Bay and Lake Okeechobee (14 feet above sea level). Glenda, Charlotte Bay. Glenda near the Manatee River. Sometimes a part of my mother would be in the picture with Glenda. A leg, half of a face. There were two blurred photographs of my mother, a gaunt, pale woman with short, grey, wispy hair and too-large dentures.

My mother died four weeks after the Florida vacation. At the funeral my father gave me her album. Glenda stood beside my father holding his arm when he said, "I love all of my children the same, but I want you to have these photographs." Davie and Sandy said that he loved me, the youngest, the best, if he was capable of love at all. They said, who wanted an album filled with pictures of Glenda Harrington. They said these things loudly, not caring who heard. On the spine of the album, my mother had taped a label. FLORIDA: RIVER PICTURES, ETC it said in black, in her definite square printing.

There was a time when my father might have liked the Saco. "What a find," he'd have said and pulled over to let us splash around and dig in the sand until he couldn't wait any longer for his next drink. Later, he'd tell his friends how he'd found this great place, best ever. They ought to go there, he'd tell them. But he'd never tell them the way.

For years now he wouldn't have noticed a river. He couldn't have seen it out of his eyes, which are faded with cataracts, bloodshot with booze. Besides, the only water he liked, he never tired of telling me, was the water he mixed in a drink, ha-ha. Then he'd hold up his glass and say, "I can give this up anytime. It's no problem for me." He'd turn and shuffle his way from the kitchen to the living room to sit in his corner of the sofa.

The sofa was darkened and sour smelling at the end he used—the left end nearest the door—and the carpet where his feet rested was worn to blackness. He kept a table near him. On it were the telephone, his cheque book and credit cards, his electric razor filled with old whisker dust and always plugged in, the remote control for the television, which he said he didn't watch though he didn't turn it off either, adjusting the volume from hearing to mute only when he had to, and several opened packages of butter cookies that he ate with ice-cream instead of meals.

After my visit last summer I swore I'd never go back. He was drunk the whole time, ignored his grandsons completely. He couldn't keep a thing in his stomach or his bowels. Brought a plastic container into the living room and vomited into it whenever he needed to. The kids spent their days at the beach, or in their rooms.

Every morning they asked, "Is Grandpa sick again?"

I answered, "Yes."

His skin was yellowed, or red and black with large fluid-looking bruises that appeared from nowhere. His ankles were thick and veiny and he cut downward slits into the tops of his socks so he could get them on his feet.

I had ten days to spend with him and I felt I had to stay every one.

On the eighth day I told him he had to eat something or he'd die, told him he should slow down on the booze, which he continued to try to drink. I never told him to stop completely. I never said, "You're an alcoholic." Or, "You have to give up alcohol if you want to live." I said, "Slow down for a while" or "Eat something" or "What can I get you?" and poured the drink weaker.

When I told him to eat, he'd answer that he could give up drinking whenever he wanted.

"Just like that!" he said, and he snapped his fingers with a sharp and definite click.

When I got up in the morning, he was in the dining room. He had the box of bran flakes and raisins poured onto the table.

He was dividing the cereal, raisins into one pile, flakes into another. He didn't look up when I said good morning, but continued to separate the raisins and flakes, one at a time, into piles. Raisin. Flake. Raisin. His face was wet and snot ran from his nose. His hands shook and he used one hand to hold the other as he made the piles.

"It's too much," he whispered. "It's too much." He laid his head down, his cheek pressed onto the smooth surface of the table, his greasy hair brushed the raisins. "I always loved your mother," he said even more quietly, "though I know you'll never believe that."

I'd heard stories about my father when I was growing up. I always believed them, even as I waited for evidence of their truth. The stories went something like this: he was the best swimmer in Victoria County. He could swim upstream in June when the water was frigid and swift and as red-black and foamy as blood. He dove from the top of the one-lane bridge which spanned the Barachois. Each dive was perfect, barely a ripple. He was a daredevil. He saved three people from drowning: John MacNeil; my mother the year before they were married; and his own best friend, Malcolm MacDonald, who died a year after the rescue in a boating accident near Little River. Malcolm was meant to drown, my father once told me. He said that he had allowed Malcolm a practice run at drowning before Malcolm finally got it right.

¤

The water is just right; sand oozes up between my toes but is solid underneath. I call to Neil and Thomas to look out, here I come. I run between them. Their squeals, shrill and healthy, are absorbed into the water as I dive under it. I let the current catch me, lie on my back and close my eyes. The water's pace becomes mine. I turn and swim against the relentless and calming force of the water. I relish the effort and the need to work.

I flop onto the sand and tell my children we're going to take a breather. We're going to find a campground, and learn a little more about the Saco. Maybe we'll climb Mount Jackson, or drive up the Mount Washington auto road where the weather can turn from good to bad in minutes. I tell them we'll get to Cape Breton soon enough. As I dive into the water again, I believe that to be the truth, or near enough at least.

Carmen Waits

Carmen sits by the window and watches hummingbirds fight. Crystalline autumn light defines her sharp nose, the cleft in her chin, illuminates her wide-set eyes. Glints off the brassy iridescence of the hummingbirds' bodies. When she tires of their fighting she looks over at her husband, Ron. Sometimes she looks down at the floor because she thinks she sees an insect skitter across the shiny hardwood. When she turns her head it is gone.

"Did you see that?" she asks Ron, who is reading a mystery novel, his favourite kind next to westerns.

"What?" he asks, but he doesn't look up, doesn't look Carmen in the eye.

Carmen has been seeing insects at the periphery of her vision all her life. Even before her mother died and Carmen went crazy. Carmen's psychiatrist had coaxed her to talk, tidied up her craziness, normalized and encapsulated her grief in two precise clinical words: situational depression. The situation was death. The depression was the hollow in the mattress where the weight of her mother's body had rested for the months of her illness. The depression into which Carmen curled herself the day after her mother's funeral, where Carmen lay until her father lifted her from her mother's bed to take her to be cured.

Carmen had stopped washing, stopped eating, stopped getting up in the morning. Carmen had stopped her periods from coming. She had stopped talking. Some days she was afraid of the rug beside the bed; some days, when she watched the curtains as they billowed on a gentle breeze coming in through the window, Carmen was sure she would die of fear. One day terror came when she saw the bedroom doorknob turn. It was not that she was afraid of someone coming in; she was simply terrified of the doorknob. She didn't tell anyone about being afraid.

On the morning he took her to the psychiatrist, her father lifted her from the pungent wrinkled caress of the sheets. He carried her to a waiting bath, gently placed her in it, nightgown and all. Then he left her, and Carmen's Auntie Norma, her mother's sister, came in to bathe her, lifting the thin wet nightgown over Carmen's head, scrubbing her like a child, washing her hair with baby shampoo that did not sting her eyes.

"Oh my scrawny sad bird," her auntie crooned. "You're just a handful of bones."

Her auntie poured water over her shoulders. "Come back, Carmen."

Carmen watched her auntie's competent hands, so like her mother's, thick soft white fingers, each almost as wide as it was long, square-cut fingernails painted the red of a hummingbird's throat. Ruby red. She watched her auntie's lips, two small bright flapping wings beating out sounds that were all the same to Carmen. "Hum, hum, hum. Hum, hum, hum."

In her head Carmen knew she loved her auntie, loved her father as he carried her out to the car, drove her to the psychiatrist's office. In her heart she felt nothing at all.

Carmen has never told anyone that she sees insects out of the corner of her eye. Especially not Ron. He already knows Carmen lives her life on shaky ground. Until just before the pregnancy she felt protected with Ron, safe. She wanted to feel that way, and Ron seemed happy enough. Then Carmen started dreaming about her mother, about her illness and death. And Carmen wasn't sad anymore. Her mother had died. It was past.

Now Carmen is ready to do some protecting. And the first thing she wants to protect is this baby inside her.

"Do you intend to work?" Ron asked.

"I'll go back when my maternity leave is up," Carmen told him. "But I might take some extra time. I've been working at the clinic for twelve years. I'm entitled to a leave of absence."

"I don't mean later. I mean now."

"Hopefully, everything will be fine, but I'm not going back to work until I'm certain the baby is safe," Carmen said.

"I won't be able to take time off after," he said.

"I never asked you to," Carmen reminded him.

Lately, Carmen finds herself provoking Ron in small ways, like the zipper shoes she bought yesterday.

Carmen likes zippers. On anything, but especially on leather. The shoes are a nappy brushed black suede. They look like Hush Puppies with thick square three-inch black rubber heels that make her taller than Ron, who is five foot five. They have shiny wide stainless steel zippers up the front.

Carmen tried the shoes on four separate times before she bought them. They pinched a bit. Nothing she couldn't stand until they were broken in. They were one hundred and two dollars without tax. But no, those weren't the reasons she hesitated. It was the fact that Ron would hate them. In the end she tried to please him by buying him a new copy of his favourite western, *Lonesome Dove*, when she finally bought the shoes.

"I have *Lonesome Dove*," he said.

"It's falling apart. There are elastics around it."

"I like it like that," he said.

"Why don't you like them?"

"I didn't say that."

"Ron," Carmen said.

"They're ugly. Why do you do it?"

"What?" Carmen asked.

"Make yourself look hard. They're slutty."

"That's what I like about them, Ron."

Carmen wears the shoes now with a sweater she bought that is the colour of illness. It, too, has a zipper. She got the sweater on sale. The zipper runs on a slant, but it shouldn't. Defective, but Carmen doesn't mind.

The sunlight from the window warms a spot on her belly. Carmen caresses the warmed flesh beneath her sweater. She would like to whisper to the baby, ask it to stay, ask it why it is threatening to come too soon. Perhaps it is defective. Perhaps that is why.

Sometimes the flitting shadows Carmen sees are bigger than insects, but she doesn't want to think about that. Insects are manageable. She is not particularly afraid of insects though she prefers not to have to deal with centipedes or spiders with hairy bodies. House spiders are fine. Ron makes her leave them alone.

"Don't kill spiders," he tells her when she gets a tissue to whisk a transparent winter spider into the toilet. "It'll rain. And they eat bugs."

Carmen doesn't point out that it's winter and unlikely to rain, or that there are no bugs in the house except for these pale thin spiders that move slowly, almost invisibly, across her walls. Because there are insects. Even if Ron can't see them. Instead she gently wraps the spider inside a tissue and carries it to the basement where she releases it, knowing that soon it will make its way back upstairs to its proper home.

Carmen doesn't like the cobwebs spiders leave. But once, over five warm spring days, Carmen watched a huge black spider build and rebuild a perfect glittering web between the stems of the plants in her garden. The spider's body was two inches long, hairy, with yellow stripes across its back. It carried an oversized woven egg sac at the base of its abdomen.

The web was strong enough to catch wasps and bumble bees, and one day a beetle the size of a quarter. The spider did not bother Carmen, but then it wasn't slipping past her on the floor faster than she could see. On the sixth day the spider was gone, its web a tattered fragment drifting on a breeze. Later that day Carmen watched as a pair of hummingbirds took strand after strand of the spider's silk to decorate their nest.

The spider had deserted the web before her eggs had hatched. It reminded Carmen of her mother leaving one day for an ultrasound to confirm an embarrassing, but exciting, unexpected, late-in-life pregnancy: no period, extreme tiredness, an abdomen that was growing rounder, more distended. She never really came home again. The pregnancy turned out to be a tumour. Her mother died within five months. Carmen was fourteen.

That's when Carmen decided she'd never have a baby. But then she changed her mind.

"Are you going to have it?" Ron wanted to know.

"Yes."

"I'm fifty-two," Ron said.

"I'm thirty-seven."

"You could have an abortion," Ron told her.

"I planned it."

"You said you never wanted to have children."

"I changed my mind," Carmen said.

Carmen had met Ron at a university lecture by the eminent orthopedic surgeon Matthew Frenton on "Alignment: The Use of Computers and Carpal Tunnel Syndrome." The lecture had been extremely technical and only two people asked questions afterwards: Carmen Lescombe, Student, Kinesiology, and Dr. Ronald Patrickson, Neurologist. That evening Ron asked Carmen to have supper with him.

Ron was thirty-seven, recently divorced. Carmen was twenty-two. After supper Carmen slept with Ron. Because she was twenty-two and why not. Because he made her laugh. Because he had a gentle smiling mouth and kisses as soft and comforting as white bread. But that's it, she told him, once and no more. She didn't want anything serious, didn't want a middle-aged man on the rebound.

In the morning Carmen awoke to the sound of water running. Ron came into the bedroom, lifted Carmen from the bed and carried her to the bathroom where he lowered her, naked, into the water. He washed her like a child, shampooed her hair, massaged her scalp until she groaned with pleasure. He didn't get soap in her eyes.

Carmen had taken psychology; she'd read about Freud. Ron talked to her while he bathed her and all she heard was a pretty hum. "Hum, hum, hum." While her body relaxed, inside her head Carmen was alert and wary. Yes, she'd read in textbooks about girls falling in love with older men, their fathers. And Carmen had to admit she felt slightly stupid, slightly embarrassed.

In her heart Carmen felt almost nothing. Not happiness. Not unhappiness. But she did feel safe.

"I don't have children. I never want to have children," Ron had told Carmen at supper the night before.

"Neither do I," Carmen had said.

As far as Carmen knew, that was the truth, for she had already had an abortion. When she was twenty-one, five months before she met Ron. The baby partly belonged to Bernie Sanderson, who had said he loved Carmen until she told him she was pregnant. Not that she loved Bernie Sanderson, or wanted to have his baby, but she did want Bernie to come to Boston with her when she went for the abortion.

Bernie had fleshy brutal lips and teeth that left faint bruises on Carmen's skin. She had been studying too hard that term, and working at a part-time job she didn't much like. She was always tired. Bernie's biting kisses kept her awake, or at least alert to the possibility of pleasure.

Carmen flew to Boston alone and was surprised, upon landing, by spring, the thick smell of it—decaying leaf mold, thawed dog shit, warming soil. Greenery bursting, bulbs already fading, tulips on stems too tall, leaning, precarious. Shedding petals like bits of old skin. It made her cry, this shock of spring, when what she'd left behind was a frigid bright late winter day, mounds of sand and salt-discoloured snow, and the cold heart of a young man with greedy, cruel lips.

Carmen didn't tell anyone where she had gone. She spent all her savings on the flight and the abortion, paid cash, went straight back to classes the morning after her return. As if nothing happened. But Carmen remembered her friend, Leslie, from high school, remembered when Leslie had had an abortion during their last term. Leslie left her hospital bracelet in her underwear drawer, right on top, where Leslie's mother discovered it on laundry day.

Leslie told Carmen that her mother called the principal's office and had Leslie sent home, due to a family emergency, her mother had said, which is what Leslie was told. "Go straight home. There is a family emergency," the principal said. When Leslie got home her mother took her in her arms and cried. "My poor darling," she said over and over until Leslie realized her mother was crying for her.

Carmen felt that if she couldn't have the kind of sympathy Leslie had, she wanted no sympathy at all.

The reason Carmen changed her mind about a baby had to do with one of her dreams about her mother. Until this dream, Carmen remembered her mother as she had looked when she was dying: shrunken, hair as short as an air force cadet's, skin so bruised and tight and thin it looked as if it would split if Carmen touched it. So she didn't. Her mother's hands, once so wide and effective, picked at the sheets of the hospital bed. Sometimes her mother gasped for breath, fish-like, lips opening and closing, useless, cracked and glistening with the Vaseline Carmen's father dabbed on them.

Just die, Carmen wanted to say, but instead she said, "Mama, don't leave me. Please."

In the dream Carmen and her mother are exactly the same age. And her mother is healthy, vibrant, her hair and eyes shining, snapping electrically, her skin thick and radiant as an autumn apple's, blushing. Her lips are full and soft, moist and smiling.

Carmen stands to greet her mother who approaches her, comes closer and closer until her mother touches her, is upon her, then enters her, becomes her. Her arms are Carmen's arms, her hair, her lips, her smile are Carmen's. Together they hum with energy, sparkle, laugh and laugh and laugh because they are so beautiful, so alive.

When Carmen awoke, still laughing, she turned to Ron, aroused him, and made love to him. Carmen was fertile, could feel it, had been waiting for the moment even as she had denied it. She wanted, alive in her, whatever bits of her mother she already carried. She wanted to see those bits in her own child: a mouth, a gesture, the shape of a fingernail, perhaps the gentle indentation where the ankle curves to meets the heel.

Now Carmen sits in her chair by the window, this clear fall light so pure and pretty it makes her want to cry.

This morning Carmen had an ultrasound. This is what she remembers of the report:

> Large intra-uterine gestational sac. Tiny fetal pole. There is a very slow heartbeat. There is a small implantation bleed. Opinion: A miscarriage may be imminent.

"The good news is that there is a fetal heartbeat," Dr. McAdam told Carmen. "That's encouraging." Dr. McAdam had pink lipstick on her teeth. "Now go home and put your feet up, Carmen. Wait and see. There's nothing you can do."

Carmen sits in her maroon chair by the window watching two vicious jade-green hummingbirds fight. Autumn light, sharp and luminous and blue, glints off the zippers of her brushed black leather shoes. Like a queen's, her feet are raised on a carved footstool. Her gentle husband, Ron, rubs his forehead as he reads his mystery novel. He cannot meet Carmen's eye.

The dream sustains Carmen. She wills this baby to live, wills it to hold to her. Wills her blood to push through the thick blue braided cord of the umbilicus straight into her baby's slowly beating heart.

Carmen waits. And sometimes she thinks she can see an insect dart across her shiny cold hardwood floor. There goes one now.

Facts About Niagara

"When one stands near the Falls and looks down, one is seized with Horror, and the Head turns round so that one cannot look long or steadfastly upon it."
—Father Louis Hennepin, 1683

Resistance was impossible. It was too late. Already Georgina's vision had blurred, her sense of smell had abated. Taste, unnecessary and frivolous, had dissolved. Hearing remained, though as aqueous, submerged echoes. External touch was superfluous; all essential sensation eddied within her.

Her heart, forgotten at her core, became the pulse of her pain, its coursing courier. Breath burst from her lungs, deluges of grunts and gasps, propelled by each crashing spasm, each rushing, rhythmical, unstoppable torrent of agony.

Georgina, drowning in the misery of labour, embraced it, became a swelling blissful cataract of pain. She was affliction; she was torment. She was this scream, this fearsome, wild, unending wail.

Then it was over. Christopher was born.

◻

Georgina surfaces from her memory of Christopher's birth exactly twenty years ago. 11:21 a.m. She looks up from her desk and watches her mother, Constance Voll, take off her coat and gently place it on the rack. Her mother is tall and trim. Erect. Her fine colourless hair, deeply parted on the right then combed severely to the left, hangs at an angle that is straight as a ruler just below her tiny fine-boned ears. But when her mother smiles, as she does now, her face appears round and happy.

Georgina smiles back at her mother, and her smile, like her mother's, is generous, seems wide and convincing. "Hello, Constance," she says. From the time Georgina was learning to speak, she was forbidden to call her mother anything but Constance.

Constance retired two years ago from her job as a veterinarian's assistant, a career she had before she married, and kept, with one vet or another, until her retirement. "I'm a working gal," her mother always said. "Never much liked the domestic arts." Georgina's father did all the laundry and cleaning after work, bought groceries every Saturday morning using the coupons he'd clipped from newspapers and flyers.

He made arrangements for Georgina to attend an infant day nursery when Georgina was seven months old. He bathed her, read to her, kissed her goodnight and tucked her in. Then her mother would come to the door, stand a moment, book in hand, her finger marking her place. She'd turn out the light.

"'Night, Georgina," she'd say and blow a kiss.

Her father did all the cooking, though there were seven dishes for which Constance could recite the recipes by heart. Georgina found them highlighted in neon pink marker in *The Fanny Farmer Cookbook* her mother gave her when she married Geoff: Eggs Benedict, Boeuf Bourguignonne, Ratatouille Niçoise, Crêpes, Chicken Timbales. And, on page 463, Princeton Orange Cake, which Constance baked for herself and Georgina every year on the birthday they shared.

"Princeton," her mother would sigh after she finished reciting all of the ingredients in the cake and the method by which to prepare it, her ritual before she helped Georgina blow out the candles. "I should have gone to university. I should have been a scholar."

Although Georgina did not think Constance was especially curious or imaginative, her mother did love facts. She memorized encyclopedic tracts and the definitions of words she'd heard at work and didn't know the meaning of. She walked around the house while waiting for supper, repeating over and over the exact words from, say, *The Book of Knowledge*, Volume 4, or *The Concise Oxford Dictionary*.

"Cataract," Constance droned. "Noun. Waterfall (prop. large and sheer, cf cascade); downpour of rain, rush of water; (Path.) eye-complaint producing partial blindness; (Mech.) steam-engine governor acting by flow of water." She'd read the definition, every notation just as it appeared on the page, until she could repeat it word for word. "*The Concise Oxford Dictionary*," she'd say once she got it right, then snap the book shut tight.

¤

Constance has come to the office because Georgina asked her to. She tried to warn her, to tell her mother the details of the ultrasound and endoscopy report, but her mother refused to listen.

"Stop. Stop. My ears are plugged," Constance yelled into the telephone. "You're not my doctor. You don't know everything."

Georgina could hear the fear alongside the insult. Her mother wanted Bruce, Dr. Malik, to tell her face to face what was wrong.

"If it's bad news, Georgina, I don't want to remember it coming from you," Constance added.

What Bruce is going to tell Constance is that her lack of energy and occasional lower abdominal discomfort is really a 3-centimetre-long cancer in her bowel. He'll tell her that he is sending her to a fine surgeon, the very best in the field, that the prognosis is good because the cancer is localized, that there are yards of bowel and taking a section will not be so bad. He'll tell her to come into the office whenever she feels the need for information or a talk, knowing she won't come. Once a specialist takes over it is a while before a patient comes back to see their family doctor. That's just the way it is.

And Georgina is just as happy she won't have to treat her mother during her ordeal. Somebody else will greet her at their office. Somebody else will test her urine, give her her shots, book her appointments. Georgina has her hands full being her mother's daughter.

Now here Constance stands, erect and severe, her eyes begging the information she has forbidden Georgina to share. When she decided to switch physicians and make Bruce her family doctor, she asked Georgina to be strictly, excessively professional, and, as always, Georgina complies.

"We're going to go to the Elvis Presley Museum," her mother says.

"What?"

"Your father and I, when we go to Niagara Falls."

Georgina's parents went to Niagara Falls for their honeymoon in 1950, a trip her mother continues to talk about, a high point in her life. Never before her honeymoon, and never since, has she travelled further than the 582 kilometres to Niagara Falls.

While her parents were there, Red Hill Jr. went over the falls in an impractical contraption made of inner tubes and fish net that he called "The Thing." They watched him die, then they stayed and watched as the river was dragged for Red's body. They saw parts of his contraption bob to the surface, joined the collective "Oh" of the 200,000 spectators.

It is the kind of drama her mother loves, the kind she'll never forget, wishes for, waits for, every single remaining day of her life.

Meanwhile, she memorizes facts, tells anyone who will listen: Horseshoe Falls is 185 feet high, the plunge pool 180 feet deep. 100,000 cubic feet of water per second pass over the crestline during daylight in peak season times, half that amount in the off season and at nights, the rest diverted for hydroelectric purposes. Georgina's parents are going for a second honeymoon for their forty-sixth wedding anniversary, a gift from Constance to her husband.

"Your father is going to find the barber who cut his hair the first day of our honeymoon, the day Red Hill Jr. drowned," her mother says as she touches her own angled pale hair. "It cost him ten dollars. A lot of money in those days, but the barber cut Frank Sinatra's hair, had his autographed picture on the wall, so the money was worth it. I sat and watched the whole thing, maybe from the chair Frank's girlfriend sat in, or Frank himself while he was waiting his turn. I should have asked. It was so exciting."

"I remember that story, Constance," Georgina reminds her mother. She particularly remembers the part where Red Jr.'s mother was heard to shout, "I want him back, I want him back," just as he was going over the falls. The next day his broken body was recovered near the landing dock of the Maid of the Mist.

"We're getting a suite in the same hotel we stayed in in '50. It's a theme hotel now. Hawaiian Room. Polar Room. Ours is the Safari Room. It has a round bed and plants and vines, a leopard-skin bedspread and lots of mirrors." Georgina whistles and rolls her eyes. "And we'll go to see the falls at night. The lights on the spray, Georgina. My God, they're the prettiest thing I've ever seen."

Georgina smiles harder, bigger, "I should take Geoff, what do you think? We could use a little romance." But the phone rings and Georgina is almost released.

"Lunch," her mother mouths and Georgina nods her head, "Yes."

Constance sits beside Francie Leblanc who is also waiting for Bruce. Francie has lank brown hair and a hard little frosted pink mouth with tiny blazing white serrated teeth set as straight as dentures in her gums. When she smiles at Constance, Francie looks feral, and even thinner and smaller than her ninety-two-pound, five-foot-nothing frame.

Francie has come because she got a death threat from her brother between 8:00 and 9:00 on Tuesday morning. "I want Dr. Malik to record it," she told Georgina when she booked the appointment, "I want it to be official, in black and white, just in case."

Francie comes in every other week to tell Bruce about her past, lately about the naughty touches from years ago that Francie's brother told her never to speak about. Francie calls Georgina once a week to ask her to write something or other on her file so she won't forget to tell the doctor.

Bruce calls Francie's name. Next it will be Constance's turn.

◻

When she goes home Georgina will forget Francie and the other patients. Their names, their pain and joy. And today she will forget faster because she is preparing a twentieth birthday celebration for Christopher: picking up a cake, wrapping presents, thinking of the right words to put on the card, grilling a steak.

What Georgina won't be able to forget is the look on her mother's face when she came out of Bruce's office. Pale as her hair, stiletto lines slicing downward, thinning her, deflating her, as though the air had been pressed out of her body.

At lunch they talked about treatments and procedures. And how to tell Georgina's father, her mother's eyes misting over then, but when Georgina reached out to take her hand, her mother pulled it away and picked up a spoon. The surgery had been scheduled for a Thursday in three weeks' time. Her parents were supposed to leave for Niagara Falls on the weekend.

"Go. It will take your mind off things. You'll be relaxed when you get back. And it will be a while before you'll be able to go again, especially if they decide to do radiation or chemo," Georgina advised.

Her mother watched her soup as she stirred it with her spoon, round and round, forming a whirlpool of tomato broth with bits of carrot and celery surfacing, swirling in the vortex, disappearing.

"I don't want to talk about it," she said.

She turned away from Georgina and began to speak. Georgina leaned toward her mother.

"Did I ever tell you about Annie Edson Taylor? October 21, 1901. She was sixty-one but she lied and told the press she was only forty-two. She was teaching dancing and wasn't getting enough customers to make a living. She figured it was better to risk the falls in a barrel than to continue living in poverty. Some people thought she was trying to commit suicide, but she told them she was too good an Episcopalian for that. It only took ten seconds. When they opened the lid of the barrel she heard someone ask, 'Is the woman alive?' 'Yes, she is!' Annie shouted, then she asked, 'Did I go over the falls?' It's a mystery, Georgina, what will kill you and what won't."

Constance sighed and turned toward Georgina. She pushed her soup away, "I'll call tonight to wish Christopher happy birthday."

When Malcolm was born, fifteen months after Christopher, Georgina felt the same as during her first labour. The only difference was that Malcolm was born after four hours, Christopher after twenty-eight.

"I'm an ordinary woman," she told anyone who asked, "simple and direct. I've broken some rules, but followed most of them. But when the contractions started I knew right away there were no rules: none to break and none to follow. I had to become the pain."

She told how giving birth was the only time in her life that she felt she was herself, Georgina Voll. That she never felt so alive. When her labour first began, she was overpowered by the force of the will of her body, but when she gave in to the contractions, stopped resisting them, let them draw her to the brink, then over, she knew exactly who and what she was, what she had to do. She felt exactly right. There was only the pulsing, cascading rhythm of pain. And this one thing to be done. Push her baby out.

Bruce Malik was her doctor when Christopher and Malcolm were born. The day Georgina brought Malcolm in for his starting school check-up, Bruce offered her the nurse's job. It was a big decision, for she had been an at-home mother since Christopher was born. She nursed the boys until they were ready to stop: Christopher when he was three and a half, Malcolm when he was almost four. She had opted for cloth diapers, which she washed herself. She prepared her own baby food, freezing it in ice cube trays: blended carrots, organic stewed puréed apricots, sieved rice and beans when they were older.

"Why do you go to all the trouble?" her mother once asked. "You could use disposables and buy prepared food. Why must you do this, Georgina?" Georgina hadn't bothered to answer.

But she did decide to take the job. She's been doing it now for thirteen years.

The door opens. Georgina doesn't look up this time. She knows who has arrived. She's that organized, writes down each appointment in the book, asks why each person is coming, pulls the files and makes sure they are up to date, that Bruce has everything he needs to satisfy his patients.

This time it is Janet Barry with her forty-two-year-old schizophrenic daughter, Christine. Christine is coming down from a quick love affair with a so-called artist and now that the love-high is passing, she needs her fluanxol. When Christine is in love she refuses all medication, help or advice. When Janet called to make the appointment she told Georgina that these affairs always ended badly. "She doesn't fall for the right sort of man," she said, "and it always ends in disaster."

Christine is dishevelled, overweight, a little manic. She has an unlit cigarette in her mouth, practically chews on the filter. Every time she tries to light it her mother takes her hand, tells her to wait until they are out of the building. She glowers at her mother, but she waits. She flicks her lighter over and over and over.

"Thanks for fitting us in, Georgina," Janet says, as Georgina gives Christine her injection. Janet's smile is rueful, Georgina's restrained. Georgina can't imagine having to look after a forty-two-year-old child.

When the phone rings Georgina isn't surprised that it's her mother.

"When is my appointment with the surgeon, Georgina?" she asks. "I forgot to write it down. Your father cried. And could you make a copy of all the reports? I'm making a file."

"We're not going to the Falls. We want to stay home and do some research. Collect ourselves. But if we were going we'd get a holy relic, a piece of hawthorn from around Fort George. The missionaries brought hawthorn bushes grown from the original bush at Golgotha. Did you know that, Georgina? The one they used to make the crown of thorns for Jesus. And here I quote, '... a study says the thorns are an Old World species that can be found growing nowhere else in North America,' unquote."

¤

As the boys stop needing her, as they begin to build their own lives, to have secrets, to have girlfriends whose bodies she thinks they must be exploring, Georgina has started to watch herself in mirrors, trying to see who is looking back. She wonders if Christopher and Malcolm ever think of her as having a body, or if she is so familiar as to be invisible to them, a presence, yes, but myopically undefined. She watches parts of herself emerge changed: rounder, fuller, less angular and definite.

Shiny reflecting surfaces attract her and she remembers this curiosity from when she was a teenager, amorphous, just becoming aware of her presence, her physical being: breasts, hair, hips, eyes and mouth, belly, buttocks, knees, ankles, feet. Swirling disconnected parts.

¤

Lately, Georgina feels pain, but not the same as when she was in labour. Sorrow. A constricting wad of it in her chest. When she gets home from work she takes off her shoes, lies down on the couch and thinks about Christopher and Malcolm. Thinks about her mother.

She cries. Great washes of tears stream right into her ears, overflow onto the cushions. Her nose runs and she lets it. She does not move until she hears the dog bark, her warning that someone is coming into the yard. Then she rushes upstairs, washes her face, blows her nose and gets on with it. Supper, conversation, newspaper, phone calls, a video sometimes, a book, maybe a game of cribbage since they cancelled the cable. The late news, lovemaking.

During lovemaking Georgina's body seems to separate from herself. She cannot imagine that sex was ever connected to making babies. Geoff was "fixed" right after they had Malcolm. Since then sex has always been safe, supposedly always for pleasure.

Georgina feels arousal, the ache of wanting, a fullness in her groin, Geoff's fingers and tongue on her breasts. But inside the cavity of her chest where her heart beats, waiting tears press and press. Press hard up against her throat, choking her. The tears release, finally, painfully, at the very moment her orgasm lifts her pelvis from the bed.

After Geoff falls asleep, Georgina gets up and lies down on the couch again, continues crying where she left off. When she is exhausted she goes back to bed. Often she is still up when Christopher or Malcolm come home from a late night out. Georgina cries so quietly that they do not notice her in the dark. Sometimes she is awake at dawn when the nesting cardinal and her mate trill back and forth to each other, awake when the rest of the street awakens and the cardinals become silent.

¤

Once Georgina called her mother, who often complained that she slept less and less as she got older. Constance said she listened to books-on-tape in the dark, turned her chair to face an east window where she watched silvery light filter into the black sky, watched silhouettes emerge from relief.

Georgina told her mother how sad she became whenever she thought about Christopher and Malcolm, that she'd tried so hard but now she sometimes wondered if she might have failed them. How they'd become distant and remote, so private, filled with secrets they no longer shared with her. She knew it was time to let them go, but it made her feel so lonely to think of them leaving.

"What goes around, comes around," her mother told her. "You were a wild one. You never listened to a word I said. You took off out west with that dope-dealing truck driver when you were eighteen and we didn't hear from you for a year."

Georgina had to laugh out loud, couldn't help it, for she remembered the truck driver, Kenny Stone, fine-boned, wavy dark hair everywhere, funny in bed, but lazy and often cruel. She'd smoked dope, dropped acid and collected welfare until she got a job as a nurse's aide on a children's cancer ward. A job she'd left a week before she left Kenny Stone lying in bed on a drizzly Monday morning in September, rubbing the curling hair around his navel, yelling, "Bitch, I don't fucking need you." On exactly the same day she'd entered university on a student loan to study nursing. Only then did she call her parents to tell them she was fine, that she'd got her act together.

"Yes, Georgina," her mother repeated. "What goes around, comes around."

¤

Georgina closes and locks the door as Janet and Christine leave. Christine's cigarette smoke drifts in on the hallway draft. It smells so good sometimes, that first fresh exhalation of smoke. It reminds Georgina of summer nights, cars with windows open, bars. And boys with bodies like gods, her own so thin and smooth and desirable.

Tempting to start smoking again. Georgina hasn't smoked since she decided to try to get pregnant with Christopher, which she succeeded in doing right after she went off the pill.

Both Christopher and Malcolm smoke. She can't figure it out. Geoff doesn't smoke, and they never allowed smoking in the house. The boys went to schools that were preachy, almost fascist, about a healthy safe lifestyle—good food, proper rest, exercise, no cigarettes, no drugs, no alcohol, no unprotected sex. The "no's" are the things her sons now love to do the most, she's sure.

Sadness is surfacing. If Georgina doesn't get out of the office soon the tears will start before she makes it home to the couch. Lately she finds it harder to confine herself to crying only when she is alone. This will pass, she tries telling herself, for how could she go on crying like this forever? But for now the tears come in movie theatres, concerts, once at the grocery store when she walked past a mother scolding her baby, and once when she was swimming, which, if she hadn't felt so miserable, would have been an interesting experience—tears in the water.

¤

Georgina does remember a different kind of pain that made her cry and didn't last. Guilt. She had sex with Bruce right there on the moss-green rug in his office. It had been coming for over a year that was filled with sexual tension and glances, the brushing of skin on skin. Once started, the real thing with kisses and tongues and clothes coming off, Georgina knew it was wrong and hated herself for being so weak and self-indulgent. But she didn't stop. She was crying before they were finished. Bruce lay beside her, his pants around his ankles, and licked the tears away. Then he stood up and put his clothes back on.

Georgina had her back to Bruce as she dressed and told him how she wanted this job, how she liked working for him— liked him—but she wouldn't allow this to happen again and if that was a problem for Bruce he should say so right now. Bruce said, "Whatever you think is best, Georgina."

They never mentioned it, though the tension, both arousal and guilt, remained for a long time. Georgina cried off and on when she felt remorse. Or terror. What if Geoff found out? What if he left her? What if he told Christopher and Malcolm?

That was years ago, but there are still times when Georgina calmly wonders what might have happened if she had decided to keep on making love to Bruce, what her life would be like now. And she feels a particular dark pleasure, a wicked and nasty delight, from knowing that her mother occasionally stands, her long thin feet so confidently planted, on the very spot where she and Bruce had made love.

¤

Not all of Bruce's patients are a sorry lot. The pregnant women, especially the first-time mothers, are optimistic and magnificent. Georgina thinks there should be a special place for them to wait, one filled with mirrors to reflect their beauty and radiance. Even Eadie Bester, who has eleven children, the last of which, she said, "came out in my pants," looks healthier and seems more confident when she is pregnant. The older mothers look youthful and vibrant, the younger ones sure and graceful, their bodies just as they should be.

After the babies are born the mothers return for shots for their babies; for reassurance for themselves. Georgina oohs and ahs, tells the older mothers that theirs is the loveliest, fattest, sweetest, smartest baby she has ever seen. That they must be doing all the right things.

The youngest mothers, the ones in their teens and very early twenties, want to hear that they are the ones who look lovely and sweet, that they are losing weight so quickly, that their hair is getting glossy and thick again. They still want to be the centre of attention. Once Georgina has complimented them, she can concentrate on their babies.

¤

One afternoon, while Georgina lay crying on the couch, Malcolm arrived from nowhere. He had stayed home from school, he said, had been in his room. He didn't seem to notice Georgina's crying, at least he didn't acknowledge it. "I wish I'd never been born," he hissed as he flopped down on the couch opposite Georgina's.

He told Georgina that she nagged him too much. He said he was going through a hard time and he didn't need her telling him about jobs and marks and helping out all the time. When Georgina asked him what he was finding difficult and could she help, he yelled, "See there you go again, always butting in. Just leave me alone. Stop nagging," and he got up and stomped out of the room.

¤

Georgina buys wrapping paper and a birthday card decorated with electric guitars. Christopher's favourite pastime is playing guitar, though Georgina has noticed he doesn't play as much as he used to. She picks up the cake in the shape of a guitar at the bakery. She and Geoff bought Christopher an electric guitar tuner, an array of new picks, new strings for the Gibson

Les Paul (cherry starburst pattern) Christopher bought with his first paycheque after he quit high school.

Georgina buys the steak Christopher asked her to cook for his birthday supper, the new potatoes, salad greens, red onions for frying. She rushes home to get them ready.

¤

These days, Georgina doesn't have to worry about Christopher finding her on the couch crying. He comes home only occasionally, and though lately he is often gentle and sweet, as if he too knows he will soon be gone forever, he just as often rants about the stupidity of a world that doesn't treat him fairly and the faults of a mother who doesn't understand.

He comes to do laundry, to pick up fresh clothes, to borrow five dollars, to make a meal. He leaves the mess, says he'll clean it up when Georgina asks him to, but when he is gone the dirty dishes, smears of sauce, cheese, crumbs, splashes of milk and juice remain, a still life of his chaos, and of his disregard.

Georgina dreads the times when her friends talk about their children. Sometimes, instead of crying, Georgina thinks up answers to "What are Christopher and Malcolm doing these days?" "Studying in Geneva, then travelling to Antarctica," she once said. "Just kidding," she quickly added when the reply was taken seriously.

Dealing blackjack. Following a rock band from town to town, concert to concert. Learning the intricacies of marijuana cultivation. Exotic dancing. She doesn't know. If they are doing something, they aren't telling her.

Georgina also listens for the telltale signs of discord in her friends' conversations. Jenny is at Concordia but doesn't like academics. (What does that mean? Georgina wants to ask. How can you be at university and not like academics? But she knows the answer will be oblique or deferred.) Shaun had to be sent money two weeks after he got his student loan, but he is making lots of lovely friends and is getting around Montreal so well. Michael has a new girlfriend who has two toddlers and seems to be a nice woman. He is getting through second year at Queen's though he is seldom in his room when his mother calls.

It is the unsaid that fascinates Georgina. All that is under the surface. But even this makes her cry, this possible failing of children who are not even her own.

¤

When Georgina gets home, there is a message on the answering machine from her mother, "Hello? Hello? Georgina, are you there? It's Constance. Georgina? I hate machines. I won't call anymore if it's a machine. We're better now, but your father has some questions for you about this cancer. Call him."

Her tone changes, warming up, "Oh, and Georgina, I was just telling your father about Jerome Bonaparte. You know, Napoleon's brother. He was the first famous honeymooner at Niagara Falls. He married a woman from Baltimore, Maryland, but the marriage didn't last, not like your father's and mine. Your father says we can go to Niagara next year. 'We'll go to Niagara next year, Constance,' he said in that big deep voice of his. He's like you, such an optimist." Then there is a click and the sound of a dial tone.

There is a second message. From Geoff. He'll be late, an emergency at the office. He'll be home in time for Christopher's celebration supper.

Christopher calls while Georgina is setting the table. His friends are taking him out for supper, he says, he won't be home. No, he probably won't stop by later, as they are going to a bar afterwards.

"Christopher," Georgina protests, "supper is almost ready."

"'Bye, Mom. I'll wake you up when I get home."

"Happy birthday," she says, but he has already hung up. The phone rings again.

"Georgina, it's Constance. Is Christopher there?"

Georgina tells her that Christopher is out celebrating with friends.

"What? I thought you said you were cooking him steak."

"I was."

"You shouldn't let him walk all over you. Don't be a doormat for your kids. Tough love, that's what they need. We've decided to give you our trip to Niagara. The room is already paid for and we booked ahead on the Maid of the Mist. I think you're looking a little ragged these days, Georgina. You could use a rest. Take Geoff. And be sure to go to the Floral Clock. I was just reading that there are 19,000 plants used every year in the Floral Clock. Isn't that something? Tell Christopher I called. Tell him I'd like to speak to him before I die."

"You're not going to die."

"Oh yes I am. Maybe not now, but I will surely die. Goodbye, Georgina."

Georgina stumbles to the couch, falls on it. She is choked with sorrow, a stinging urgent press of uncried tears. She shudders. Wracking spasms, one, then another and another, shoot up and down her body. Her muscles knot. Pain stabs her calves, slashes her thighs, crashes across her shoulders, sluices down into her wrists, into her hands and fingers.

Georgina screams.

She screams and cries and screams.

Then suddenly she is laughing. Painfully—rasping and hard—but purely. Wildly. Laughing.

She gets up and gathers some of the birthday preparations, puts them on a tray and carries it to her bedroom. She lifts the covers from her bed, lays out her surprises one by one on her crisp clean sheets—cake, potatoes, salad, fried onions. She lies down, pulls a blanket around her, flicks on the TV and begins to eat with her fingers, wiping them occasionally on Geoff's pillow. She does not get up when she hears the dog's warning bark.

¤

When her mother and father went on their honeymoon to Niagara Falls, her mother was eighteen, her father twenty. Her mother's period started as they checked into the hotel. Constance liked to tell how Georgina's father had to go out to a drugstore in his wedding suit and buy Kotex for his bride. As he was coming back up to her on the elevator, which was crowded with people, the bag ripped and there he stood, a young man with confetti in his hair holding a box of Kotex. A groom who was definitely not getting any that night.

Georgina thought that Constance liked to tell this story to embarrass her, to remind her that she knew about the dark and intimate parts of Georgina's body. And that in this profound and inescapable way, they were, mother and daughter, alike.

The second part of the Niagara Falls story Georgina figured out herself. Nine months and two weeks from their wedding day, on her mother's nineteenth birthday, Georgina was born.

¤

Georgina eats salad with her fingers; oil drips down her chin. She knows what she's going to do. She's going to Niagara Falls. Alone.

She'll walk at night, look long and steadfastly upon the falls, see the lights on the water and in the spray. Take the room with the round bed and the leopard skin bedspread, the one with all the mirrors to piece together and watch the parts of her surprising, ever-changing body.

She'll ride the Maid of the Mist in a blue plastic raincoat with tourists and honeymooners; visit Louis Tussaud's Museum, Marineland, the Criminals Hall of Fame. She'll find the barber who cut Frank Sinatra's hair, and ask him to give her a trim, no expense spared. Look into the corners of the room to see if the shadow of her mother lingers there. Leave a big tip.

She'll ride the Spanish Aero Car above the Whirlpool, watch for a woman named Annie to sweep by in a barrel. Later she'll search the bushes around Fort George for hawthorn relics, tape bits of woody stem to postcards and mail them to her mother and father, to her husband and to her sons.

And if she must, Georgina will weep. She will let her tears become the whirling, constantly churning water that crashes over that ancient and slowly eroding cliff.

Clafouti aux cerises

Judith carries sadness in her like this November morning, brittle and stark, with no immediate hope of relief. It is the day before her fiftieth birthday and she's alone in a hotel room overlooking Lake Ontario, which is a mirror, a shiny luminous reflecting glass spread straight out to the horizon. When she told Leo she was going to Toronto, she didn't tell him when she'd be home. And Leo didn't ask.

Last night Judith had supper with her oldest and best friend, Franny Kress. Franny had been married three times and almost married one other time besides. She believed in marriage, she told Judith. And fidelity. What she really believed in was fidelity. If she couldn't be married and monogamous, then it was better to get a divorce.

"No affairs," she said. "I don't believe in affairs." Then Franny had raised her eyebrow and winked at Judith, "I also don't believe that you've never been tempted to leave Leo for another man."

"Never! No!" Judith said too fast, too emphatically, even though it was true. "If I did leave Leo, I'd never get married again," she'd added. She was a little drunk, but she believed this to be true too.

When Judith mentioned that she did look in the new phone book every year to see if her old boyfriend, Gary Berwick, was still listed, Franny had laughed and laughed.

"I bet Leo's had affairs," she said. "He's repressed but there is something sexy about him. Those shoulders," she hummed, "and just a hint of cruelty around the mouth."

Judith had told Franny that this trip to Toronto was her birthday present to herself. They'd ordered champagne and finished the bottle, drinking toasts to friendship, and to health. When Judith reminded Franny that next week was also her and Leo's twenty-fifth wedding anniversary, Franny had seemed surprised.

"Holy shit." She laughed, and raised her glass. "I'll never see one of those." Later, when she hugged Judith good-bye, she whispered, "Has it really been that long?"

¤

Judith walks to the window and looks out. The pale water is flat, steely. Although now and then a gentle wind whiffles its surface, once the breeze has passed, the water seems more ominous than before: limitless and remote. Unapproachable.

What Judith didn't tell Franny was that she needed to get away to decide once and for all if she is going to leave Leo. The crisis is immediate, a sudden unshakeable sense that this is it, she's turning fifty and she'll have been married for a quarter of a century. If she doesn't leave now she never will. She'll feel bound to Leo for the rest of her life.

She has no illusions. Leo has fallen in love twice since Judith married him. Two times she was aware it was happening, that is. The first time, just after they bought the house on Margaret Avenue, was with a temporary secretary from work. The whole business was so classic and mundane it made Judith embarrassed for Leo. The test was whether Leo would continue to be in love when the secretary's term was up. It was one thing to love someone when you could see them every day at work. It was another to have to make the time to love them: to arrange a secret lunch, a clandestine movie, a night in a motel. That was an affair. That was the test Leo had to pass or fail.

Leo wasn't a lady-killer; he wasn't classically handsome. He had pearly soft blonde hair, thinning even when Judith first met him when he was twenty-seven, she twenty-five. He had smallish pale blue eyes, pale lashes and brows, an ordinary mouth, except that it had a provocative way of stretching beyond its limits when he smiled. He had perfect teeth.

He was medium build, medium height, with nice legs, a flat tummy and a tight, well-muscled man's bum. Leo did have a particular energy. When he spoke, his whole body opened up, changed. His face became fluid and alarmingly handsome, his arms and hands caressed the air in an elegant mesmerizing dance. He leaned into his words, making them seem more intimate than they were, making the mundane particular. When he stopped talking, he became ordinary Leo again.

It was his back that set him apart. Judith first saw Leo at Sauble Beach. He was sitting in front of her on a red striped towel with a wisp of a woman with breasts like two perfect apples glued to her chest, a deep tan and a crimson bikini the exact same red as the towel. The woman was rubbing suntan oil onto a bronzed broad shouldered back on which each muscle was fully defined. Not in an over-bound way, but exactly, precisely, apparent. A perfect anatomical picture covered in a most glorious silky sheath.

Judith met all of Leo at the beach dance at the casino that very night. Alone, Leo looked fidgety, swept his eyes around the dance floor. (Later Judith learned that Leo could not stand to be alone. It made him nervous. He had to have someone to talk to, someone to stand beside, someone to protect him from appearing to be unattached.)

She'd been watching Leo from the corner of her eye, so she stepped slightly away from the crowd she was with and smiled a big inviting smile, not directly at Leo, but somewhere over his right shoulder. Leo looked around, then at Judith who had stepped back into her group again.

Next thing she knew he was touching her elbow. "Do you want to dance?" he asked. She could feel the heat from his sun-warmed skin as she walked with him to the dance floor. She placed her hand on his back, on the muscles near his shoulder, spread her fingers wide, then brought her fingers together again. They were married in November, four months later. Lust at first sight, Leo still says, after almost twenty-five years.

Leo's back is hairless, the skin smooth and shiny and always, even in winter, a little tanned. Judith likes to lie on her side and stroke the skin on Leo's back, to brush it with her finger tips, with her lips, with her tongue. To hold her body against it and feel its heat and silkiness. She misses Leo's back when he is away from her, or she takes herself away from him.

Virginia. That was the secretary's name. Leo said it over and over, slipped it into every conversation as many times as he could. It was pathetic. He didn't hear himself, wasn't even aware that he was saying Virginia this, Virginia that.

"You're in love with her," Judith said to Leo.

He didn't skip a beat.

"No, I'm not," he said. "I think Virginia's nice. I like her. She's invited us to have supper at her house this Friday. I said we'd come."

"Did you?" Judith asked.

But Leo was already on to how Virginia's daughter was away with her grandparents. How Virginia was going to cook a classic French meal. Beans sautéed with garlic in bacon fat, some meat with butter, marrow and wine sauce, and a surprise for dessert. How Virginia, along with all her other stunning traits and varied accomplishments, was French from France on her mother's side. And how Virginia was moving to a new office the following week and this was her chance to cook a thank-you and good-bye meal for Leo, who had become her friend, her only friend, in the office.

When Leo and Judith arrived at Virginia's house, Leo kissed Virginia French style, on both cheeks, then followed her everywhere she went. He even stood up when Virginia was going to the toilet and began to follow her there. He was only a little flustered when he realized his mistake. He waited in the doorway until Virginia returned, then sat right next to her on the sofa, his leg pressed against hers, his hand accidentally brushing her knee when he spoke.

Judith would have liked to leave right then, and Paul, Virginia's husband, would have liked that, too. When Virginia asked Paul to get wine for everyone he went to the fridge, took out one beer for himself, poured it into a glass and walked out of the room. When he returned he sat very close to Leo, glared at him, asked questions he already knew the answers to, like, "What did you say you did for a living?" "Do you have any children?" Then, "What does Leo do when he's not following Virginia around like a puppy dog? When do you think he'll start humping her leg?" This last to Judith when Leo had gone with Virginia to get more wine.

The meal was delicious, Judith had to admit. Everyone drank far too much. Once Paul settled down there was an artificial hilarity to the conversation, a burlesque of manners. Though they were drunk enough to let the charade continue, sometimes, when Paul looked at Judith, she saw the sadness in his eyes.

Supper ended with clafouti aux cerises, perfectly browned and delicate, the cherries big and ox-blood red in their bed of yellow custard and sugar. Judith realized she was in trouble when Leo brought her a copy of the recipe hand-written by Virginia. This was two weeks after Virginia had moved to her next temporary placement.

Leo became slightly less voluble about Virginia for about a month, then while getting ready for bed one night, he told Judith that she'd left Paul. She'd taken their daughter, Jacqueline, and moved into a new apartment which she'd rented, had signed the lease for, even before the night of the supper. He told her that he'd helped her, that's what he'd been doing the Saturday he said he was helping a friend from work move.

Paul was furious and was going to try for full custody. He thought Virginia and Leo were having an affair, which he thought could be grounds for a custody suit. Leo seemed shaken by this. He seemed bewildered. How could Paul think this about his and Virginia's friendship, that they were lovers?

Judith felt that if Leo was telling her this he wasn't yet sleeping with Virginia. Touching her, kissing her, but not yet sleeping with her. She also realized that Leo didn't even know how in love he was with Virginia. But Virginia knew, and perhaps she'd put more store in Leo's love than she should have. Perhaps she should have waited to get the apartment. Waited until Leo had said out loud that he loved her, so that he could hear the words and then they would have been fact.

Two months later, Leo told her that Virginia had moved home, that she and Paul were trying a temporary reconciliation. Judith felt sorry for Virginia and was almost grateful to her for having shown her what a repressed soul poor old Leo was. Leo, who Judith thought was an honest person, had not been dishonest; he'd been stupid. She felt it was good to learn this about a husband.

Judith also kept the ingredients for clafouti aux cerises in the house at all times. It was an obsession, one she never mentioned to anyone, not even Franny. This reminder: two tins of large Bing cherries, pits in. Eggs. Cream. Flour. Sugar for dusting the top.

Leo became quiet after Virginia moved back home. He became sulky and lost his appetite. Once Judith made clafouti aux cerises for him, partly to see if it would tempt him to eat, partly to see what he'd say.

"What did you make this for?" he growled in the tight nasty way he had when he was interrupted from an engrossing task, or did not like the service he was getting in a restaurant, or a bank, or a department store. "I didn't ask you to make this."

Leo went off sex for a while, too, giving in occasionally and servicing Judith, or at least that was how Judith felt when he turned over onto her, bounced around a few times, grunted and rolled off. Judith knew he was back to normal when he came to her while she was bathing one night, brought her a glass of armagnac, sat and talked about his day.

Sometimes Judith asks Leo if he remembers when he was in love with Virginia, but he tells her it was all in Judith's head. He liked her; they were friends, but that's all there was to it.

The second time Leo fell in love was more serious. Claire was a sophisticated smart woman, a woman from Judith's office who she found attractive herself. Tall and graceful, Claire wore tasteful clothes with just a touch of eccentricity that made her seem exotic. She had large breasts and a small waist, curly auburn hair that she sometimes let go wild; other times she tamed it into a bun or a French roll that was never tight or prissy, but loose, as if it was just about to come undone, though it never did.

Why she chose Leo Judith wasn't sure; all kinds of men practically begged Claire to notice them. Judith believed Leo didn't at first. But with some help, eventually he did.

Judith knew that Claire had affairs, mostly with married men. She knew of one marriage for certain that had broken up because Claire had decided to have some fun. At least that was how it appeared to the wife left behind. In the end Claire never married the men she took from wives.

Eventually the men left Claire and went home. Before long they left their wives again to marry younger women. Women more conventional than Claire. They had second families, went to prenatal classes, despite having been in Belgium or the Yukon when the children from their first families were born. They coached soccer, went to ballet recitals, hockey games, parent-teacher interviews. Doing it right this time, they said, yes, this time they were going to get it right.

Their ex-wives remained single, or had sad affairs with married men who never left their wives because they felt that they had to act responsibly, that their rebelling teenagers needed them, that their jobs required propriety. That intact families were better than broken ones, no matter how unhappy they were.

The signs were the same the second time as the first. Claire, Claire, Claire. But this time there was a reserve, as if Leo had become more cunning, or wasn't quite sure what he'd got himself into. He became dreamy, lost in reverie while doing chores, while reading the newspaper, even while making love to Judith. She knew he was somewhere else because he said things about her, how soft her hair was and his hand would touch the air around her head but never actually connect with her.

Judith had just had her hair cut into a drastic, spiked, butchy style that suited her sharp features and her just-starting-to-get-rounder forty-two-year-old body. In daytime Leo told her he thought her haircut was a bit daring, that he wasn't sure he liked it, it would take some getting used to. He said he liked her hair best when it was long, the way she wore it when he first met her.

Leo became sentimental. Nostalgic. When he talked to Judith it was as if she were someone he hadn't seen in a long, long time. He recounted what his life had been like, reminded Judith about their son, Sam, how he had learned to walk or talk. How Sam used to say the sound an animal made, instead of the word for the animal.

"What's that?" Leo would ask and point to a cow.

"Moo, moo, moo," Sam would answer.

Leo laughed at the stories he told. He was gentle with Sam, clapping him on the back, asking him how he was. How was school? Did he have rewarding friendships? Sam was a teenager and surly, and looked at Leo as if he had just stepped off the moon.

That was the year Judith's father died, and her mother, who had multiple sclerosis, had to be placed in a nursing home. That was the year Sam started drinking and taking drugs and lost interest in school. And that was the year Franny had surgery for breast cancer, then chemotherapy, then radiation, and lost all her hair.

Leo remembered when he and Judith were first married, how they ate pizza from boxes and drank rye whiskey with ice and ginger ale. How they made love in every room, on every surface. They made love on beaches and in the water and in a pup tent in P.E.I. in the middle of a thunderstorm so the crashes and booms drowned out their cries of passion. That was the very night Sam was conceived.

In bed he was gentler than he had ever been, asking Judith did she like this or that, what did she want to do, did it feel good when he touched her here or there. But in between it was Claire, Claire, Claire.

Then as quickly as it had started, it stopped. Claire transferred to Montreal and married a lawyer from a reputable family, whose ex-wife had three angry grown-up children. Claire was Catholic, so the lawyer had his marriage annulled. Leo and Judith were invited to the big church wedding, but they didn't go. Leo said he didn't want to. Prior commitments, he wrote on the reply card.

When Leo stopped saying Claire's name he became himself in most ways except that he took on everything he could at work. His hours were longer, he travelled more, he didn't take all of his holidays in a year. This became the pattern of their married life. It was not an unhappy marriage, but it was a set one.

The one thing that didn't change from the Claire period was Leo's gentle lovemaking. He remained tender and thoughtful and grew in passion and dexterity and experimentation so that sometimes when they were finished Judith wondered could this really be Leo, her Leo, or was this another Leo, molded by different experiences in another life and placed here in her bed for her enjoyment.

Just once Judith asked Leo if he had slept with Claire. She and Leo had finished making love. Leo was lying back, his hands behind his head. He was awake but not talking, not even acknowledging that Judith was there. Leo said no, he hadn't, but there was a bit of a pause, a trace of hesitation, as though he wanted to say something more. As though what he wanted to say next was that he had slept with her. Or maybe that he wished he had.

But Leo never overtly hurt Judith. The hurting, the pain he inflicted, he never acknowledged causing. If he hadn't known he was in love with Virginia, if he could say out loud he hadn't slept with Claire, then his life was one of clarity and honesty. He could live with himself.

What brought her to Toronto was the one she didn't see coming. On arriving home from work a month ago Judith listened to the messages on her answering machine. They were the usual: call Penny at the gas company now and save on the spring furnace and duct cleaning. Call Franny, she would be in town on Friday. Two calls for Sam.

The final message was from a woman with distress in her voice. "If you have a husband, he is cheating on you," she said. That was all. "If you have a husband, he is cheating on you."

Judith sat down. Some things began to fall into place. Over the last few weeks a woman with wispy brown hair had taken to riding her bicycle up and down the lane-way, stopping to look over their fence into the yard if no one was outside. Judith had watched her drive by one afternoon when she was bringing groceries in from the car. She was pretty in a worn sort of way, tall, not thin, not heavy. She wore casual clothes, the kind bought at expensive outdoor sports specialty shops. When she saw Judith she stared at her, then looked straight ahead. She didn't acknowledge the polite nod Judith gave her.

Then there were the late night calls where the caller hung up when Judith answered, but not right away, always with a second or two of hesitation, and not before sighing. Finally, thinking this was someone getting some kind of weird kick, Judith handed the phone to Leo. Leo answered, listened for a while to a voice that actually spoke to him.

"Don't ever call here again," he said into the receiver, and handed it back to Judith. The calls stopped.

"If you have a husband..."

¤

It is September; Judith is twenty-five. She's sitting on the couch in her apartment leaning back into Leo's arms. The heat from his body emanates through his clothes, warms her. Leo breathes into her hair, rests his cheek on her head. They've been drinking, but they're not drunk. They have made love, but are dressed again. Leo's going back to his apartment soon. They aren't married, in fact it's not in the cards. Leo hasn't asked, and besides he's just accepted a job in Vancouver and will be leaving after Christmas. Judith has a good job. They'll write. They'll see each other on holidays. They'll visit.

Leo begins talking quietly, whispering really. Though she cannot see his face, she feels his words caress the back of her ear, the warmth of his breath on her skin. His first serious girlfriend came to see him this past spring, just before he met Judith, he says. He hadn't seen her in years. They were very young when they met, became very close; she wanted to get married, but Leo wasn't ready to settle down.

She was distraught when they broke up. Some nights she called him, always late, and cried on the phone. Some nights he watched her walk back and forth in front of his apartment building. She told him he'd regret his decision. He didn't hear from her again until the night she arrived at his door.

She was getting married the next afternoon at 2 p.m., she told him after he let her into his apartment. She came because she and Leo had never slept together. Tomorrow was her wedding day, so it was now or never. Leo took her to bed; they made love all night long. She left in time to appear to have awakened early at her parent's house. She was going to tell them she hadn't slept well, she'd gone for a walk, she was nervous.

Leo says he doesn't know why he's telling Judith. Judith asks him how he could have slept with his old girlfriend; what about the wedding, what about the husband-to-be? Leo says he doesn't know him, has only seen him around a few times. Judith asks him, "Don't you feel guilty?" Leo says, "No." Judith says this makes her feel jealous, and very uneasy. Leo says, "You don't have to be jealous. She's married now."

"Besides," Leo says as he turns Judith to face him and kisses her on the lips, "I'm going to marry you."

Justine and Rockette

Always travel lighter than the heart.
—"Packing for the Future: Instructions"
Lorna Crozier

In January, Justine began wandering the aisles of grocery stores. She returned misplaced items to their rightful homes. They were waiting to be rescued, she thought. Like her, they were marooned, red onions weathering tinned ravioli storms.

And it was in January that Justine began to mutilate bread. Before Terry left, but during the time she knew he was going, their love a waning moon almost invisible. She bore a constant indefinable weight in her chest, which drew her shoulders down and pressed into her arms, made them heavy. Every time she came to the bakery aisle the weight spread into her wrists, pushed her hands toward the aromatic white bread, its flesh so soft, so inviting.

Each slender loaf fit within the spread of her wide palm. Her fingers wrapped over its edges, around its sides. What next but to squeeze? So she squeezed and squeezed and squeezed. The bread yielded. Then gently, ever so gently, she placed it back on the shelf.

Each time she crushed bread she felt the thing that had been her heart, the weight that took up all of the space in her chest, begin to contract. And she would sigh, air forced from her lungs as if it was her last breath. A prayer-like exhalation: My heavy heart. My sinking heart. Oh, I'm losing heart.

"Stop it!" the baker shouted the last time Justine crushed bread.

"What?" Justine asked, and she looked the baker in the eye. His eyes were blue, almost turquoise, the same shade as the sky-and-sea icing on the children's birthday cakes. She turned to leave.

"You're hurting my bread," the baker wailed. He picked up a crushed loaf, dangled it like a football from his hand.

She began to run down the bakery aisle toward the cash registers and the electronic door.

"Everybody squeezes bread," she shouted over her shoulder.

The door popped open. The baker followed her, then stopped. The door closed behind him.

"It's your handprint," he said, and he turned the bread in his hand like a dying thing, then cradled it in his arm.

"Don't come back!" Justine heard him shout as she closed her car door.

¤

Terry left in February. Now it is April and instead of mutilating bread, Justine checks the due date slips in the back of library books. It doesn't hurt anyone. She doesn't read the books. These days fiction puts her to sleep. Non-fiction is too real and sad. Or too harrowing.

What she likes is the texture of books, their heft, the cool feel of a just-turned page against her cheek. She likes the sharp lines on the due date slips, the dates contained in neat black rows. An orderly list of expectation, of fulfilled responsibility. A hopeful progression through time, so patient, almost tender.

One of the books she took out of the library yesterday was published in 1993. The library received it in September. Six people took it out that year. Seventeen in 1994. Four in '95, six in '96, two in '97, two in '98, none in '99. Now it's April 2000. Justine took the book out just so the date could be stamped in it. She and Rockette are going to return it later today, after Justine finishes some letters for Marco.

This morning Marco dropped off thirty profiles for letters. Marco runs an international adopt-a-foreign-child rip-off.

"One more year and I'll be able to retire," he told Justine as he set the profiles on her desk. "Freedom fifty-eight."

Marco places ads in local papers throughout North America to link do-gooders with foreign kids. The kids are fakes, figments of Marco's imagination. And Justine's too. Marco pays her poorly.

"You're complicit, Justine," he tells her if she complains about the pay. Twenty cents a word. Sweatshop wages.

"Why do you work for Marco?" Terry used to ask her. "He pays you shit and the work's illegal. It could get us both in trouble."

Terry works for an investment firm: Andrews, McAuley, Trope. Justine had worked there too, researching new technology companies. Until she moved in with Terry and he worried that it might appear to be a conflict of interest if they both worked at the same firm, in the same office. Terry always worried about the way things would or would not appear.

"I'll switch to ventures," Justine said.

"I'll support you until you find a new job," Terry promised, appearing to be a supportive lover.

Justine said, no, she'd find a job, and she'd use her savings to pay her share of expenses until she did.

But she didn't find a job. And she used up all of her savings. Terry did support her. For a while. Until she asked him to stop. Until he started to complain and make Justine feel as if she wasn't doing enough to find a job. Until she started a company writing letters and résumés, and helping clients to set up business profiles and to design advertising flyers. But there were never enough clients and there was never enough money. Until Marco came along. That's when Terry really started complaining.

Marco collects the proceeds from the adoptions and banks them in a special account. He uses some of the money for travel to exotic destinations where he takes photographs of the poorest people he can find. Field work, he calls it. Making sure everything is running smoothly. He managed to obtain charitable status, has the required number of board members (all friends, some of whom travel on the organization's account, too). He hired Justine to look after the paperwork. Marco invents the profiles of the kids: family, country of origin, circumstances. He pays Justine to type these, and to compose and type the letters from the children. "They need a woman's touch," he said.

He brings her onionskin paper, slightly musty and a bit stained. All the letters are typed on an old Underwood with a sticky "p" and "r". Dear Hampton Family, a letter will begin, the outline of the "r" and the "p" a reverse Braille, shadows pressed into paper. The paper smells like mildew softened with a hint of wood smoke and sandalwood.

"The Body Shop," Marco told her when she asked about the sandalwood. "Do-gooders love sandalwood from The Body Shop. Reminds them of their hippie days. Wood stoves, dope, incense and shit."

¤

Terry told Justine he was leaving while they were watching a documentary about hurricanes on TV. Justine's hand was on Terry's thigh. He was petting it absently. On the television screen a weatherman reported that a hurricane was passing through Miami. The picture flashed to a man with a hockey player haircut who told them he had thought he was going to die that day. He'd prayed to God to spare him, then he'd given up.

"I resigned myself to dying," he reported. "I knew it was the end."

He had a video camera, so while he waited to die he filmed the storm. The film is shown. The wind was fierce—yowling—and clouds boiled in the sky. Rain blew horizontally. The walls of the man's house creaked and bowed.

"I'm moving out, Justine," Terry said as the walls of the man's house began to crack.

A scientist appeared on the flickering TV screen, pictures of air masses forming and re-forming on the monitor behind him.

"A hurricane is of tropical origin. The development of instability is dependent on an air mass becoming saturated. This is called conditional instability."

Justine slipped her hand from Terry's leg and tucked it between her knees. She turned sideways on the sofa to watch him.

"I'm moving in with Bonnie Seguin. I didn't want to tell you until we were sure. I didn't want to hurt you. But Bonnie said no matter when I told you it was going to hurt." Terry didn't take his eyes from the television screen.

"How very thoughtful of Bonnie," she said to Terry's ear.

"It's not Bonnie's fault. And it's not just Marco and the fake kids, Justine. It's us. But if you want my opinion, you should stop working for Marco. Find a real job."

Justine remembered meeting Bonnie when she still worked at the firm. Pale. Small boned. Excessively feminine. Constantly wiping her nose. Justine turned to watch the TV again.

"Clouds align themselves in rain bands," the scientist continued. "The rain bands spiral toward the storm's centre where they wrap themselves around the eye."

The top of the storm funnel shown on the TV looked like water speeding over Niagara Falls. A mesmerizing relentless cascade.

"Is Bonnie going to quit work for you too?" Justine asked. "I think she should. That is, if you want my opinion."

The TV flashed back to the film of the man who thought he was dying. The wind still blew; the rain still fell horizontally. The roof was flying off his house piece by piece. "Oh God!" they heard him cry above the shrieking of the wind and the renting of his house. "Oh God, oh God, oh God!"

Then there was silence on the screen. The night sky appeared. There were more stars than Justine had ever seen before. A few skinny cirrus clouds passed under them. Gentle breezes shifted the curtains of the man's destroyed house.

"The air smells like yeast," they heard him shout. "Praise the Lord, praise the Lord. There is pure starlight straight up to God."

"After the wall of the hurricane passes," the scientist said, "you will meet the eye. Within the eye the winds are light and the clouds mainly unbroken. The inner eye is an essential element in the life cycle of a hurricane. This deceptive calm can last for up to one hour before the inner wall of the hurricane arrives and continues its destructive path over the surface of the earth."

"Bonnie is allergic to dogs. I can't take Rockette," Terry said.

"When are you leaving?" Justine asked. But she was thinking yeast. She was thinking bread. How soft it was, the luxurious happy smell of it in the bakery.

It didn't matter when Terry left, for she had been getting ready for his leaving for some time.

¤

Marco is clean-shaven and balding on top. He wears his remaining hair in a dyed black ponytail that he tucks into his shirt collar when he's trying to look businesslike. He wears black turtlenecks or cotton shirts with Nehru collars, sporty jackets and pressed black jeans. Very believable. Very art-film-directorish. He came on to Justine the day after Terry left. Leaned over her while she was typing, put his hands on her breasts, kneaded her nipples. Justine looked down. The tears running from her cheeks dripped onto his liver spots.

"You're old, Marco," she said, hoping to wound his pride.

"You're an attractive woman, Justine," he told her. "You can't blame me for trying. I wouldn't be the man I love if I didn't try."

"Fuck off, Marco," Justine told him.

Marco stores the onionskin paper in sealed plastic bags with a cloth soaked in sandalwood oil, another permeated with wood smoke, the pages tucked into brittle, water-damaged books he buys at flea markets and garage sales.

"If you ever find old library books with due date slips, will you bring them to me?" Justine asked when Marco told her about the old books.

Justine has two books, DISCARD stamped along the pages, little pockets in the back with due date cards tucked inside them. The dates on the cards are hand-written: Jan. 26, 1932; Mar. 14, 1932; April 04 (her birthday) in script so pretty she thought of having a tattoo copied from them. Tiny willowy peacock blue dates circling her ankle. A numeric history, impersonal but attached to someone, somewhere who'd been inspired. Or not. Regardless, the book passed from person to person, week by week, year by year. Impervious to criticism, to bad decisions, to being discarded.

¤

Justine decides to forget Marco and the fake letters today and walks with Rockette to the library. It's spring and unseasonably warm. Rockette loves spring, its rot, its awakening smells. She sniffs and paws at a dirty pile of melting snow, dislodges an almost petrified piece of decaying roadkill. A bit of squirrel, or someone's cat, a tuft of black fur and bone. Just enough flesh to leave a black mark near Rockette's collar when she rolls on it. She stands and shakes, then prances, head high. She's impossibly happy. Justine ties her to the bike rack and goes into the library.

As she does every day, Justine sits at a study carrel near the self-help section. There are eight carrels in a row, a low barrier separating one from the other. She waits. When the man beside her stands and goes to the washroom, Justine stands too, then moves to his carrel and looks at the books he has left open beside his binder. She closes each book, looks at its title, and puts it into her cloth satchel, which cost one dollar: Support Your Public Library, it says. There are four books: *Diet and Heart Disease, Recovering from Your Heart Attack, Mending Broken Hearts: A User's Guide*, and *12 Steps to a Healthy Heart*. She goes to the checkout counter.

As the librarian stamps her books, Justine can hear Rockette protesting, yipping her displeasure and loneliness outside the automatic doors. Justine wishes she could do that, sit outside Terry and Bonnie's door and yip. Terry had left no forwarding address or, yes, Justine would be tempted.

This morning Marco had shown her a picture of a tiny brown-skinned girl. Four at most, Justine thought. The child's shift was the colour of oatmeal. Black hair, black eyes, fine red dirt dusting her feet. She held a rag with button eyes, nose, and mouth.

"This is Maria. She's six." (They argued about the age. In the end Marco won.) "She has four brothers and one sister. Her oldest sister works for the local priest, as does Maria's mother, Margarita. Maria's father was killed in the floods of '99."

Most days Justine would rather be doing anything than typing these hard-luck stories, these tales of woe. Laundry. Trimming Rockette's toenails. Vacuuming. Anything.

¤

When Terry left he took the vacuum cleaner, but he left Rockette, his fine yellow lab. She's a little on the heavy side. Even though Justine walks her to the library every day, it doesn't seem to help Rockette's weight. Justine used to hate how Rockette needed Terry to be close by, hated her yowls and cries when they left her alone for more than two minutes, her silly snorts and smiles when they reappeared. Now she's sympathetic. Now she understands exactly how Rockette feels. Abandoned. Every two minutes she feels abandoned.

A haze of yellow dog hair covers the rug. The rug is all that's left in the living room. Terry took the sofa and matching chair, the end tables and lamps, the bookshelves, books, CD player and CDs. They were his, of course. He had asked Justine to get rid of her things when they moved in together. He'd get rid of his. They'd have a fresh start. Why shouldn't she do as he'd asked? She was in love. She was optimistic. She trusted that soon she'd be working and able to pay Terry for the new furniture they were buying.

Justine's desk and chair, the typewriter Marco brought her, her computer and one lamp are in the bedroom. Terry took the bedside tables and the bed frame. He left the mattress because it had bloodstains from Justine's periods.

Rockette sleeps with Justine on the mattress on the floor. Every night Rockette sniffs where the bloody spots are hidden beneath the sheets. Justine once read that a dog locked in a room with its dead master would eat the master within four days rather than starve. So much for the starving, loyal-dog-on-the-grave theory. Likely waiting four days to dig up the rotting corpse, have a feast. Funeral food. There is yellow hair on the blanket on the bed, too. Terry took the kitchen table and chairs, the pots and pans.

The rug in the living room is navy blue. More celestial than navy, really, as there's a touch of purple, a hint of grey, a little bit of first light in its shading. Bright yellow constellations are scattered across it: Orion, the Big and Little Dippers, the North Star, Taurus, Castor and Pollux, Mars and Venus, the moon. A rug artist's rendition, for the confluence is not on any star chart Justine has found in library books. When Justine painted the living room walls she continued the night sky theme, using dark blues along the baseboards, lightening the tones as she painted up the walls so that by the time she reached the cornices, the night sky had become dawn, which then became brilliant sunshine. Electric blue and azure shifted into the white of cumulus clouds that drifted across the ceiling. It took her a month to finish but even Terry was impressed when she was done.

Sometimes she and Terry smoked a joint, lay on the rug on their backs, pretended the clouds had shapes: a sheep, a snow-man, a tree. The Tragically Hip played in the background—Courage, it couldn't come at a worse time. They ate mango slices, dark chocolate, clementines. Made love. The dope made Terry's skin feel like the cool smooth surface of an eggplant.

Terry had left her the car because it was Justine's, in her name. She bought it while she was still working at Andrews, McAuley, Trope. As a research assistant. A Toyota Corolla. 1986. White except where the rust is. And the duct tape, which holds various parts in place, mostly mirrors and the left front bumper. A Red Green vehicle. A Tom Green joke. But it goes.

The car smells like Rockette when she's wet. Old fish and damp woolen socks. Like Justine's hockey bag. She hasn't played in two years. Something else she gave up for Terry. He said he felt emasculated—his word—by Justine's hockey playing. By her proficiency at defense, her occasional goals, by how loud and vulgar her team was when they came over for a beer after a game.

Lately, on really bad days, Justine opens her hockey bag. Like Rockette, she's trying to get oriented, trying to locate the memory of something primal and necessary, some scent that will help her find her way. On really bad days she takes the still sharp blade of her skate, runs it along her cheek. Runs it along her cheek. Runs it, along her cheek.

¤

When she arrives home, Justine checks the due date slips—four books, sixty-one due date stamps, an average of 15.25 each—and puts the books back into the bag to return them to the library tomorrow. She washes Rockette in the bathtub, scrubs the black mark from her neck, rubs her dry with one of Terry's old towels. She brushes her on the celestial carpet. Rockette breaks away, runs around in circles, shakes and rolls. When they're finished there's so much hair on the rug, Justine decides to clean it. Without a vacuum cleaner.

It takes six hours. Until 3 a.m. She uses her hairbrush, pulls the hair into little piles. She whisks each pile onto Maria's photo. The hair is electrified, ignites Maria's fingers, her lips, the button eyes of her rag doll. Then Justine licks her fingertips and lifts, one by one, each stray hair left on the rug and places it in a paper bag. She decides to save the hair as her mother once saved the clippings from her first haircut. She was three; her sister Joy was six. One envelope each.

June Winowski's Hair Salon. Gerrard Street. 1980. That's what her mother wrote on the envelopes. Joy Helen Morrow. Justine Blanche Morrow. Justine writes Rockette on the outside of the bag. April 2000. She seals it with tape.

Terry left Justine's high school graduation dance picture, too. It flies from under the mattress when Justine strips the sheets and blankets from the bed and throws them onto the floor. Rockette circles the pile, sniffs it, lies down and groans. She's still damp, her hair bright and fluffy. She smells like shampoo: sweet, bubblegummy.

Justine tips the photo to the light. In it she looks like a candle: straight floor-length white dress, yellow hair piled high like a flame, the lick of red on her too-big lips glowing at the centre of her face. She went to the dance with Len Brebner, who looked like a sandwich loaf. A too-tight brown suit encasing his pale soft flesh. He couldn't kiss but still they necked until their lips were swollen and sore. Two days after graduation Justine moved to Midland, took the bus and stayed with Joy and Joy's brand new husband Tony.

Justine slept in her sleeping bag on a webbed aluminum chaise longue in the storage room in Joy's apartment. When she went to the Employment Centre to see what jobs were available, the woman told her she shouldn't have come, she should have stayed in Toronto. She was going to take jobs away from people who'd lived in Midland all their lives. She didn't deserve a job; she was selfish. Justine left, shamed, and cried all the way back to Joy's. The woman must have been having a bad day. Maybe her husband had left her. Justine thinks these things in retrospect.

She did find a job. Through the newspaper. At a credit company that went after people who didn't pay their funeral expenses—flowers, urns, plots, etc.—or their dental bills. That was their specialty: cremations and cavities. On Fridays at lunch the staff went to La Roma to have hot meatball sandwiches, drink the house red, laugh and tell stupid jokes about root canals.

It was honest work. But sleeping beside Joy and Tony's bedroom night after night, listening to their sighs and moans, made Justine lonely. For Len Brebner? Or maybe for kissing? She went back to Toronto. She found a good job, bought her car. She met Terry and Rockette. Terry Harper, star broker of the investment firm. On the rise, risen and gone. Rockette, overweight yellow Lab. Jilted, now living with Justine.

¤

Rockette gets up. Her nails click-click along the hardwood floor as she comes toward Justine. She places her nose under Justine's arm and nudges. Justine takes Rockette's face between her hands and blows softly into her gentle dog's nostrils. Rockette licks Justine's face, then crawls up beside her on the mattress and falls instantly asleep. Justine holds Rockette's ear between her fingers, the underside silky and cool. She rubs it absently. Rockette sighs. Dog sighs, deep and optimistic: Take heart. Your heart is in the right place.

Justine bends and kisses the top of Rockette's head. Then she stands, and she inhales as if for the first time, filling her lungs with a pure, cleansing, limitless breath.

¤

That afternoon at the library, as Justine was untying Rockette from the bike rack and Rockette squirmed and snorted and smiled her ingratiating grin, the man from the study carrel had burst through the automatic doors.

"You took my books," he shouted. "Give them back."

"It wasn't me," Justine protested.

"The librarian said you took out four books. I had four books. You took them, I know you did." The man's face turned a dangerous shade of red.

Rockette began to bay. She pulled at her leash, jerked Justine away from the man.

"I have to go," Justine said over her shoulder. She was crying. She felt ashamed, but she couldn't give the man his books. She needed them. "I have to go home. Can't you see that my dog needs me? I just have to go home." She whispered this to herself, and to the warm spring air, for there was nobody left to listen.

¤

Justine leaves Rockette asleep on the mattress and goes into the kitchen. She cleans out bits of food from the refrigerator, puts them in a trash bag and carries the bag to the garbage chute. Rockette is waiting for her at the door when she returns.

Justine packs one bag for herself and another for Rockette—
Rockette's bowls, her food, her leash. She grabs Marco's profiles.
She takes the bag of library books. She and Rockette leave the
apartment.

Justine throws the bags into the car and sets the profiles on
the rear window ledge. She drives to the library and returns the
books through the night depository. She gets into her car and
heads north. She is going to Midland to visit Joy. It's a start. She
won't stay long. But there's lots of nice scenery on the way.

The windows are down. It's still warm, though there is a
hint of winter threatening to return. The sun is rising, a great
glowing lemon in the brightening sky. There are black clouds
building to the north. Rockette sits on the seat beside Justine.
She is grinning; her tongue lolls to the side. She lifts her head,
licks her lips and sniffs the air. As they accelerate onto the
highway, Marco's onionskin tragedies drift out the back windows on the slipstream.

Yes, they're on their way to Midland; they're leaving the
road maps behind. Instead Justine will trust this dog, and this
faint fresh scent of hope. They will encounter the storm ahead,
weather its inevitable fury. And still they will arrive, get there in
their own good time. Tired, less lonely, more lighthearted. More
lighthearted for sure.

Sunflowers

This is my first memory: I'm with my parents visiting my aunt and uncle—my mother's brother and his wife—in Rosedale, Ontario. It's April, sometime just after my third birthday. I'm standing in the middle of a puddle. My feet are cold and wet and I'm wearing brand new shoes. My parents told me not to get them dirty.

"You don't want to get your new shoes dirty," they said, first my father, then my mother. Then they sent me outside to play.

I stand and wait, see the thin white slivers of ice at the edge of the puddle. I watch as my parents and my aunt and uncle file out the door. I watch as they line up along the porch rail. I wait to see what they will do. I'm calm, not at all afraid. I don't smile.

What does this say about me? I'm not sure, but I think it must be significant. In all of the photographs taken of me when I was a child, I never smiled.

¤

My father used Gillette razor blades in his stainless steel razor. He placed the used blades, slightly green along the edges, in the slot on the bottom of the Gillette package. He slipped the fresh blade into the groove of the razor head, then tightened the twin flaps by twisting the razor's handle.

I liked to watch him shave. First he washed his face with soap, then he heated a washcloth with steaming hot water and held it to his skin. He wet his face again and lathered Noxzema onto it. Noxzema smelled astringent and cool. We used it for sunburns in summer. He only ever used Noxzema for shaving, because he'd had acne as a young man. It went away when he started shaving with Noxzema. When I inherited my father's acne he suggested I wash with Noxzema. It didn't help.

Often the things parents suggest don't work. It's all hocus-pocus anyway, trying to get rid of acne. Everyone has a theory. You never know what will work, but most things don't.

When I was six I opened my father's razor and took the blade from it. I held it in my right hand and made a neat slice beside my knuckle on the inside of the baby finger of my left hand. At first there was a perfect cut, a thrilling deep line, white and thin, about an inch long. A brilliant crimson seam welled along the line, then obscured it. Blood ran from the tip of my finger; it ran down my arm and dripped from my elbow. I shook my hand. Droplets flew about the bathroom: red on the white sink, red on the white toilet, red on the white walls. Splashes of red streaked the mirror, pooled on the floor.

I screamed. My mother ran to me. "What did you do to yourself?" she asked over and over. "What in God's name did you do?" Only then did I think that the cut should hurt; it must hurt. I can't remember if it did. But in the end this memory is about the wound, not about the pain. I still have the scar, my first.

¤

I like the sunflowers in my garden. I like their gaudy brilliance and their razzmatazz, their stand-up-tall flirtiness. Every day they shout: look at me, look at me. Chartreuse, banana, lemon, chrome-yellow.

¤

Yellow flowers are associated with death and are only appropriate for funerals in Latin America.

The Gardener's Companion

Frida Kahlo painted her face within a sunflower.

"I don't like the idea. I seem to be smothering inside that flower," she told a friend.

She took a knife from her bedside table, a knife inscribed with an obscene saying, and scraped her face from the sunflower's centre. (Listen. Can you hear the sound? Sharpened metal on old dried paint. An eye destroyed, Frida's full lips, her thick dark eyebrows like a crow's wing across her brow.)

In photographs, Frida rarely smiles. When she does she places her hand in front of her mouth to hide her blackened teeth.

¤

I was twelve when I broke my right arm. My mother asked me to take a group of neighbour children, and my own younger sisters and brothers—I am the oldest of nine—to the pioneer museum in Doon. It hadn't yet opened for the season, so we turned around to go home. But my mother wasn't expecting us for hours, so we had lots of time to dawdle. On our way home we stopped beside the cliff in Cressman's Bush.

"You love to boss people," my sisters and brothers tell me, but I think I most loved to boss them. My sisters say I had long fingernails and liked to scratch them if they didn't listen to me. I don't remember, but it's possible.

"Get away from the cliff or you'll fall. Stand back," I ordered.

If I ordered them around it was because my mother had put me in charge. What else was I supposed to do? I would be responsible if anyone was hurt.

Pushing in front of them, I turned to face the damp air that rose up the cliffside from the Grand River. I slipped. I thought I was running, at least my legs were moving rapidly, but only occasionally did the tips of my toes actually touch the ground. Each faint toehold propelled me faster and faster down the slope. I struck a small tree, flew into the air and landed on the riverbank.

I remember arriving home in the stranger's car my brothers and sisters had flagged down. I remember ruining a brand new-to-me, second-hand, blue vinyl car coat. I remember lying in a hospital bed covered in mud, crying over my coat.

My mother said, "It's all right. I can wash the coat."

The orthopedic surgeon's name was Dr. Talon. He knocked me out and set the break, which he said was very bad. He wrapped layers and layers of tensor bandage around my arm, a new technique, then strapped my arm firmly to my chest by wrapping more tensor bandages around it. I had just begun to grow underarm hair, a few thin wisps; I had just begun to perspire. Soon I smelled. My mother bathed me. I was grateful to her but I hated her. Because I was helpless, and because I was twelve years old.

Still, I felt special. Like Nancy Drew, I'd had an adventure. In school I wrote with my left hand. The scribbles looked foreign and exotic.

¤

In 1987 I learned to ski. Though a competent skier, I could never relax. I felt a sense of panic as I skied down mountainsides, air rushing past my face, boards on my feet, sticks in my hands, as if the poles could help prevent me from hurtling to my death. I stopped skiing in 1992. I offered no excuses.

¤

Vincent Van Gogh painted sunflowers one summer in France.

"How beautiful is yellow," he said.

Just after the winter solstice, he sliced off his ear with a razor, wrapped his bleeding flesh in a handkerchief and gave it to a prostitute.

"He's not completely mad. It was just the lobe," Vincent's brother Théo told his wife Johanna as he read Vincent's letter aloud.

Sunflowers were Vincent's study in brilliance, his high yellow note.

"Well, my own work, I'm risking my life for it, and half my reason has gone," he wrote to Théo.

¤

My sunflowers are a gift of sorts. First I fed sunflower seeds to winter birds—redpolls, purple finches, blue jays, chickadees. Greedy and careless, they dropped many seeds into the snow beneath the feeder. Scavenging squirrels hid these seeds beneath the snow in my garden. In the spring thirty-two seeds germinated. Unplanned pregnancies. They crowded my chives and rosemary, my iris and sage and yarrow. They shaded my cosmos, dill and fennel, made them grow too tall, too quickly, and fall over.

¤

Do not send yellow flowers in France;
the colour stands for infidelity.

The Gardener's Companion

Vincent and Théo went to Paris and dipped their sticks into the honey pots of prostitutes. They contracted syphilis. They shared it with others; Théo shared it with his wife, Johanna.

Frida wasn't in Paris, but in Mexico, when she told a friend that she didn't bring a virgin hymen to her marriage to Diego Rivera. She'd been in a streetcar accident when she was a teenager. She said that a pole pierced her uterus and emerged through her vagina. At least that's how she told it.

"That's when I lost my virginity," she said.

Brave Frida, passionate Frida, bathed in blood, her clothes stripped away by the force of the accident, impaled on a metal handrail. Onlookers called, "Help for the little ballerina."

One passenger carried a bag of gold dust. It burst upon impact and gold sifted over Frida's bleeding naked body, her brilliant sunburst body set on a chrome stem.

A janitor from her school recognized Frida and pulled the rod from her body to the terrible sound of cracking bones. (Hear them, so like the bones the neighbour's cat crunches as he eats the redpoll that lingered too long under my sunflower seed feeder.)

¤

When I was sixteen I was propelled, head first, through the windshield of a car. My body flew out the window as far as my hips, then slammed back onto the seat. I was sitting sideways talking to my friend Jane, who was driving. We had just seen a movie at Fairview Mall Cinema. We were supposed to be studying for exams. The car slid on ice: freezing rain. It was November.

I didn't know we were sliding, but I knew something was wrong. I could see it in Jane's eyes, wide and frightened, but by then we were driving straight into a hydro pole. We weren't wearing seatbelts. Who did in 1967?

Glass sprayed over us and over the seat. The steering wheel snapped. Its jagged edge cut a hole in the knee of Jane's pants. I had nicks and cuts all over my brand new full-length brown leather coat, which I'd paid for myself with savings from my part-time job at Zehrs. There were thick gashes in the leather, across my shoulders and over my hips.

"Shit, shit, shit," I said. "My coat."

Blood ran down my neck; it tickled me. Someone helped Jane out of the car. Someone else opened my door but wouldn't let me get out. I saw horror in their stare. In fact, there were people everywhere, most just walking by and staring. Someone offered me a cloth for my head.

"Why?" I asked.

They placed the cloth against my temple, held it there. I had a sensation—not unpleasant but odd—that my head was huge, that if I tried to touch it, I'd have to reach past the ceiling of the car.

I felt happy. When the ambulance came I asked if we could travel with the siren on. I thought it was terribly funny to be going to hospital in an ambulance.

"My parents will kill me," I said. "I wasn't supposed to go to the movie. I'm supposed to be studying."

I explained to the attendants that my parents were at a Christmas dinner for the employees of Weston's Bakeries, where my father worked. My mother had a new dress and sling-back stiletto-heeled shoes. She seldom went out to dinner.

I had my head shaved over and around the cuts. A surgeon, who told me he was at the same movie I'd been to and had driven past my accident, sewed together the flaps of skin on the side of my head. He removed glass, slivers of which, even now, make their way to the surface of my scarred temple. I worry them out with my fingernails.

I missed my exams. My mother brought my leather coat to the hospital.

"Look," she said. "It saved your life. All these cuts would have been on you."

I wish I still had that coat.

¤

The squirrels return for their stashes. Where each was hidden there is now a flamboyant yellow sunflower flaunting its fecundity. These happy sluts want sex, more and more of it: this bee, that wasp, the quick, soft rub of a butterfly's wing. Indiscriminate. And still I love them. I want them for myself. Whenever the squirrels get too near I set my dog on them.

"Get them," I yell to the dog, whipping her into a frenzy. "Get the squirrels," I scream like a pimp protecting turf.

¤

Frida was a teenager when she decided to become Diego's lover. He was in his forties, fat and married. He left his wife, married Frida, then was unfaithful to her. So Frida was unfaithful, too. Diego divorced her, then married her again a year later. Frida cried, but still she sewed his underwear, huge underpants made of coarse cotton which she dyed shocking pink. Often she embroidered them.

¤

Every year on his birthday I take my husband's photograph. He stands beside our bed in fresh underwear and holds up his fingers, or a card, to show how old he is. He never smiles. He tracks the yearly changes in his body: the shift of flesh, the firmness of it. I think he has changed little; my body has kept pace with his—our sags, our jowls, our wrinkles—so I never notice profound differences.

What I do notice is how our bedroom has changed, our double bed with the quilt my grandmother made for our wedding is now a queen-sized bed with a bright duvet, a Matisse-like print. Yellow, red, blue and green flowers. The bed is covered with pillows in bright flowery cases. Billowing curtains hide the once-stark window. Golden yellow carpets warm the once-bare floor.

¤

Vincent never became a husband; prostitutes were his intimates. And painting, of course. And for one summer he painted sunflowers, then went mad. I don't know if he sewed his underwear, but he did cut off his own earlobe.

Georgia O'Keeffe, like Vincent and Frida, painted sunflowers. Before the desert and the bones, but after she'd married Alfred Stieglitz. Georgia sewed her own clothes, all black, but didn't sew Alfred's. Nor did she embroider his underwear.

"Alfred always insisted on wearing a certain kind of tie, a particular type of sock and underwear and shirt. I used to have to walk all over town trying to find the special kinds," she once told a friend.

Though this must have been tedious, she didn't go mad or cut off her ear. In between shopping for underwear she painted, and sometimes she painted sunflowers.

¤

My dog snarls, her hackles rise like razors, so stiff, so terrifying. But she's not effective. The squirrels retreat. The squirrels return. They scrabble up a stem, quickly gorge themselves on the ripening seeds. They scurry away when I open the door.

The dog has begun to tire of the game. She's become bored, moves half-heartedly and turns to see if I'm watching.

My sunflowers are ragged; some are broken. They lie with their fallen companions the cosmos, fennel and dill. Their hearts have been eaten out.

¤

Just before Christmas, the year I was thirty-three, I had surgery for cervical cancer. In situ, a reassuring term. The surgeon cut away a cone-like section of my cervix, but not before I told him that my sister had haemorrhaged when she had this same procedure. The bleeding couldn't be stopped. She almost died. Her surgeon took her back into the operating room and removed her uterus. My surgeon didn't listen when I told him this story. He wasn't the other surgeon, the incompetent one. His patients didn't haemorrhage.

I haemorrhaged. Clots the size of oranges formed beneath my wounded cervix, slipped like small soft babies from between the lips of my vulva. I felt each one, the feeling at once sensual and terrifying. Flop, flop, flop, flop out onto the towel my husband helped tuck under my buttocks to absorb the blood.

My husband called the hospital. The nurse asked to speak to me.

"How many pads an hour are you using?" the nurse asked.

"I'm not using pads," I told her. "I'm using bath towels."

"I need to know how many pads," she said.

"I'm not using pads," I repeated, then I relented. "About one a minute," I lied.

Firmly, as if she'd known this all along but had to wait for the correct answer, she told me to come directly to the hospital.

My surgeon was surprised to see me, but he jovially stuffed yards and yards of gauze into my vagina. He sent me home and told me to come back the next day and he would remove the packing. I went back and he removed it, unwinding more and more bloody bandage into a pail. As he got closer to the end, rich bright red blood oozed out despite the cloth. The nurse held the pail under my buttocks to catch the blood as the doctor stuffed yards and yards of fresh gauze back into my vagina. He sent me home.

"Leave the packing in for three days and come back," he told me.

All the packing and repacking worked. The bleeding stopped. That year I reclaimed my maiden name. Midnight,

New Year's, 1985. I wanted my name, not my husband's, on my grave when I died.

¤

Frida died at forty-seven, one-legged, broken. Diego gave her extra sleeping pills near the end. Eleven or so. Enough, though that's not all that killed her. Heartache and alcohol helped. After she died, Diego locked himself in his bedroom and cried. No more Frida. No more sunflowers. Certainly no more handmade underwear. He told his friends he'd had no idea he'd miss her so much.

Vincent, when he was thirty-seven, took two days to die from a gunshot wound to his stomach. He shot himself. Oh, he must have loved to suffer, or hated to, one or the other. He smoked his pipe as he waited for death. Perhaps the pipe's heat and bright blazing core reminded him of summer, his high yellow note. His sunflowers.

Georgia lived to be ninety-eight. Shopping for underwear for Albert must have been a proper exercise, an appropriate break from painting sunflowers. Later there was the desert air and a young lover. And painting, of course, always the painting.

It could be said that I've given up the fight to save my sunflowers. Last night there was a hard frost; this morning the dog snores on her bed, her legs twitching, her paws running. She dreams of summer and the thrill of the chase. I let her dream and fill the bird feeder for the first time this year. I'm careful to spill many seeds onto the ground, easy pickings for the squirrels.

Two of my beauties survive. I see them now from the window. They are as garish as ever. They flaunt their glory and ignore peril. I envy their disdain. It seems less frivolous as November nears.

I am forty-eight. I've wounded myself, I've been wounded by accident, and I've consented to being wounded to save my life. I've borne two sons and had cancer in the cervix through which they were born. I've suffered a broken bone and several broken hearts and recovered. I've had stunning sex, and some sex that wasn't so fine, but I've never had syphilis. My husband buys his own underwear and poses in it on his birthday. My ears are pierced but are otherwise intact. I don't paint.

In April I'll be forty-nine, middle-aged for sure. But it will be spring, so who cares? If the squirrels haven't helped me, I'll plant my own seeds, a random spread, and wait once again for the heat, and the sunflowers, and the fecund gaudy brilliance of summer.

Intervals Between Wars

Each of us wished to have a homeland
free of neighbours
and to live his entire life
in the intervals between wars.
—"One Version of Events,"
Wislawa Szymborska

Every Friday morning Sandra massaged warmed oil into the knot of scar tissue at the base of Ursula's skull. She used the circular motion Ursula preferred, small orbits spiralling outward. She moved her hands downward, massaged Ursula's shoulders, across the flayed yellow-grey skin, which puckered and stretched, first smooth, then lined and mottled, like the plucked carcass of an uncooked chicken.

Ursula was born in Dresden. Before the war. True-blooded, she liked to say, blonde and blue-eyed. Now her hair has no colour at all. And her eyes, the sudden blue of breaking light on her good days, are often pale and clouded with pain and narcotics.

"Aryan," Ursula whispered to Sandra this morning. "That's a bad word now."

She giggled like a child.

"I gave Hitler a bouquet of flowers when I was seven. During a parade. I was picked from all the girls in my school."

Ursula pointed to herself, grinned, her eyes big and round.

As Sandra covered the portable massage table with a fitted flannel sheet, she glanced at Ursula. Ursula puffed out her chest, lifted her chin.

"Me!" she said more loudly—very loudly—and she pointed again, stabbed her finger into her soft breast.

Her voice was so insistent Sandra turned to her. Ursula looked straight into Sandra's eyes until Sandra turned away.

"Hitler kissed me on the forehead. It was like electricity. I felt it go all the way down my spine. It made my scalp and the soles of my feet tingle. It was from that moment that my visions began."

Ursula touched her head. She closed her eyes and began whispering again.

"Mama was so proud. She called me Hitler's child. 'Du bist Hitlers Kind,' she'd say. 'Du bist Hitlers Kind.'"

Ursula opened her eyes and waited for Sandra to respond.

"Lie down on the table, please."

Ursula shuffled over, obedient baby steps, her feet never lifting from the floor. Sandra took her hand, the fingers almost blue, nails long and shaped and painted a fleshy pink, and helped her up onto the table.

"The Jews..." Ursula began.

Sandra undid Ursula's gown and pressed hard—too hard— into the hollow at the base of her skull.

Ursula stopped speaking. Sandra started.

"Victor Klemperer lived in your hometown during the war. In Dresden. I've been reading about him. Did you know him? He thought he was a Protestant, was baptized one, but it turned out he was a Jew."

Sandra slid her fingers up and down the sides of Ursula's neck, more gently now that she had the upper hand.

"He wrote a memoir about the war. He said in it that the Gestapo arranged substitutes in advance for every Jewish transport. They assumed, correctly, that a number of suicides would occur. 'German organization,' Klemperer said."

Sandra massaged Ursula's tense shoulders.

"He loved being German. I wonder if he was at your parade?"

¤

"I'm not finished with you."

Sandra steps toward her son Peter as he thuds up the stairs, giving her the finger as he passes from sight.

During supper, Sandra had tried to convince Peter to stay in school, to finish this year at least. Peter has just told her to get off his fucking case.

"Come back here."

His door slams. The walls shake.

"Right now."

Music thumps alive.

"Now."

Sandra chases up the stairs, jerks Peter's door open.

"I said, we're not finished."

Peter lies on the floor, the dials on the stereo beside him jump, hit the red. He flicks his lighter, watches the fire, his face as bland as a news announcer's. He passes his finger through the flame.

Sandra reaches over and turns the music down. Peter reaches over, turns it up, all the while flicking the lighter, watching the flame. As Sandra moves to turn the music down again, Peter looks right at her, his eyes dark fathomless pools, almost lifeless. He holds his finger in the flame. Holds it there, five - six - seven - eight - nine - ten - eleven.

Sandra grabs the lighter and leaves.

¤

Ursula's shoulders are fleshy, pale. Between them, at the base of her neck, begins a line of twisted skin, a bulging layered wad of shiny scar tissue that runs the length of her back.

When she was a young mother, Ursula was in a car accident. A metal rod was inserted into her spine and continues to cause her the most outrageous pain. She takes a cocktail of drugs—Darvon, Tylenol 3s, something for sleeping, Naprosyn to relax her muscles, and Lithium for her unliftable depression.

Sandra imagines the drugs might kill an ordinary person, but what she must try to do, once a week, is distract Ursula from her pain, make her skin and muscles and crumbling bones believe, even if just for a short time, that they are vibrant and healthy. Free of pain. Sometimes, because she is good at what she does, Sandra succeeds.

¤

While Sandra and Peter fight, Karl paces back and forth in the kitchen. Karl always paces during Sandra's and Peter's fights. One time Sandra's sister-in-law Janice told her that Karl used to pace when their parents fought, too.

Except once, Janice said. Karl was twelve and she was six. Things were really out of hand. Dishes shattering, the dull thump of fists on flesh. Karl stopped pacing, she said. He walked calmly as you please between their parents, demanded money for a movie and treats. Told them he was taking Janice out of there.

They stopped fighting and gave Karl the money, turned to watch as he dressed Janice for winter. Took her hand.

Janice didn't remember what movie they saw, hated not remembering, but she remembered Karl rescuing her that one time.

¤

Sandra comes downstairs and throws Peter's lighter onto the counter. Karl stops pacing and gets himself a beer. Pours it into the one and only glass he ever uses, a university tankard emblazoned with his fraternity crest, "KARL" spelled out beneath it.

"I don't know where that boy came from," Sandra nods toward the stairs.

Karl looks in the direction of the nod, not at Sandra. He sets the tankard down on the counter and absently shapes crumbs left from supper into a square. He makes the square into a straight line. Sandra watches.

"Two speeding tickets in two weeks. Failing, now saying he's quitting school. The kid's nuts. What do you bet he asks for the car tonight?"

Sandra waits. She wants to hear Karl's voice. To hear the anger or fear or hate in it.

Karl sighs, pushes the crumbs into a line again, then a rectangle, then picks up the dishcloth and wipes the counter clean. He grabs his beer, takes it to the living room and sits down on the couch. He cracks the newspaper open.

Sandra follows him, sees the paper, his fingers like sausages wrapped around the sides. Sees the top of his head above the paper, his legs beneath. She sits beside him. Presses her leg against his. Presses hard. Thigh to thigh. Waits.

"What?" Karl says. He crosses his leg away from Sandra's. He doesn't lower the paper.

"No-fucking-thing. I'm going to bed."

¤

"You're worried about your son."

Ursula's voice was muffled as it rose from the table. Sandra would have liked to ignore her.

"I can tell."

Ursula is psychic. From the Hitler kiss, she believes. She's told Sandra tales of her visions—true and terrible, or at times comforting—and what she's seen of other people's lives. She does it for money, though if she sees danger she'll give the information free.

Sandra had never mentioned having a son. Peter. And, until this morning, Ursula had never commented on her life, for which Sandra had been grateful.

"I said, you're worried about your son." Ursula lifted her head from the table.

When Sandra first took Ursula as a client, she'd asked her about her children, did they live nearby?

"I don't have any."

"But it says on your chart you have three."

Two daughters and a son. And a husband. It turned out that the husband had deserted her. She'd placed the children in temporary care after the car accident. With her injured back, she was too incapacitated to look after them. When she recovered enough to go back to work, she signed the children into permanent foster care without ever seeing them again.

¤

When Sandra leaves Karl sitting in the living room drinking his beer, she goes to her bedroom, the one room in the house she has decorated for herself. A room where she spends more and more time. The bedroom walls are a thick, drying-blood red. A womb tone. The bed is huge, the frame intricately carved cherry wood: dragons, unicorns, broad-boughed oaks, bunches of grapes still attached to the vine. The mattress is covered in luxurious duvets with bright flower prints. The sheets are deep red; the eight pillows covered in red, blue, gold cases are strewn carelessly. Two sea-blue reading chairs sit on a thick red carpet.

Low dark blue shelves are crammed with books and photo albums filled with Peter's mementos: school pictures, hand-drawn greeting cards, first haircut trimmings, report cards, baby teeth.

At the end of the bed is an antique travelling chest, smooth pale nickel strapping over scratched misty-blue leather. The chest is framed inside with age-darkened aromatic cedar; the walls are papered, water stained, and so old a pleasant mustiness mixes with the sweet scent of the cedar. Sometimes Sandra lifts the lid just to smell inside.

Now the chest holds Sandra's favourite clothes, washed, pressed, ready to go in a flash. In the time it takes to say goodbye.

It also holds a cardboard shoebox filled with small articles that Sandra has stolen from her clients: A miniature ceramic cardinal from Madeleine Frayne, a paraplegic. A Legion tie pin from Bernard MacNeil, whose legs are still filled with shrapnel. A plain Royal Bank calendar of Ursula's with each day of each month marked off with one black line, top right to bottom left, ruler straight.

¤

"You're ignoring me," Ursula said very quietly.

Sandra preferred to work in silence, allowing the rhythm of the movement of her hands and the needs of her clients to define her pace. Sometimes, if she had a particularly chatty client, she diverted conversation with a tape of soothing music.

New Age stuff she never listened to otherwise: Vivaldi's Four Seasons interspersed with the sound of waves lapping against a shore, or the hum of insects and distant bird calls, or the whisper of breezes as they passed through the leaves of trees. She wished she'd brought a tape today.

"Sandra."

"I'm concentrating on your muscles."

¤

Sandra's fingers are long and straight, ringed with faint wrinkles, new in middle age. Her slightly ridged nails are a healthy pink, trimmed short and filed cleanly so there are no rough edges. No protruding slivers to scratch or nick a client's skin. The backs of her hands are broad and strong, faintly reptilian, tendons raised, ropy blue veins mapping the area just beneath the surface. A constellation of irregular pale brown freckles has just begun to spread above her knuckles.

Her palms are rectangular, large. Bigger than Karl's when they pressed their hands together to compare. That was a long time ago when she and Karl still touched each other fearlessly, in awe and in wonder.

Her love line is long but broken. The life line—a deep crease—extends from her wrist, across her palm, then wraps right around the edge of her hand. The line that rules her head is also long, slopes downward toward her wrist, but has several branches, an omen that she is destined to worry, and to suffer.

There are a few scars: an accidental run-in with a piece of broken glass when she was a child has left a ridge along the top of her thumb. A thin white line marks where a cleaver nearly severed the top of her ring finger while Sandra chopped carrots for a stew, and daydreamed about the baby growing inside her.

She'd called to Karl, then sat on the floor, her arm raised in the air, blood dripping from her elbow, her head pressed between her knees. She'd shivered.

Karl came at once, applied pressure and cleaned the wound. He bandaged it and mopped up the blood. He poured Sandra a glass of wine, and brought her a blanket and a pillow.

Sandra lay on the floor of the kitchen near Karl's feet, curled into a ball, hugging her finger tightly between her thighs. Her wound throbbed to the beat of her heart. She watched Karl's feet move, first to the sink, then to the stove, and back again to the counter, domestic paths, the gentle swish-swish of his beige corduroys comforting.

"Talk to me while I finish your stew."

Karl wiped the blood from the knife and began to slice carrots. She chattered into the air around his feet.

Later, when the cut had almost healed, Sandra removed the bandage to expose it to the air. Karl held her hand in his, looked at the scar.

"Our first wound," he said. And he kissed it.

¤

Sandra wears no rings. She placed her plain gold wedding band on the kitchen shelf six weeks ago. She put it there after a fight. Not a fight really, for Karl hardly spoke, but stood across from her in the kitchen looking out the window. Sandra'd asked Karl if he'd consider seeing a counsellor with her. And later with Peter. Karl said she could go if she wanted to, but he wasn't going. It would end up being about him, he said, and not about them. He was sure of it.

"A make-Karl-better session," he said, and he looked at her for the first time. "Because you're right, Sandra. You're always right about everything."

He said this so fiercely, with so much anger and hate, that Sandra felt as though she'd been hit, that the pain she was feeling in her heart had transferred itself to her bones and muscles and skin, making them feel bruised and tender. Swollen. Her clothes too tight, hurting her. Her ring strangling the blood flowing to her finger.

¤

Sandra worked on Ursula's buttocks and the tops of her legs.

"You're wrong, Ursula. I'm not worried about anyone." She was lying, of course.

Sandra did worry about Peter. And Karl. And herself. She wondered if she would ever completely disown Peter the way Ursula had disowned her children. She might, she thought. If he wanted her to; if he came to hate her that much. Or maybe because she was cruel. Or because she lied. She didn't know anymore. She had decided to leave Peter with Karl. With her gone they might begin to talk to each other. Yes, she was sure they would. Still, though Sandra thought it was the only thing that could save them, maybe it was just an excuse.

¤

"Where's Mom?"

Peter stands in front of Karl, his feet almost touching his father's.

"In bed."

"It's only eight o'clock."

Peter moves his right foot to nudge Karl's.

"Can I have the car?"

The question sounds as though he just thought of it.

Karl snaps his newspaper.

"It's just going to sit there all night anyway. I don't get it. Why can't I have the car? You're just so..."

It's quiet. The quiet goes on and on.

"You don't even have the balls to say no, do you?"

It's not a question. Peter's voice is adult and sad. Worn out.

The door slams. Windows rattle.

Sandra's been listening from the bedroom.

"Why didn't you talk to him?" she yells.

She knows Karl won't answer. He'll pretend not to hear her even though you can hear everything through the walls and ceiling, or up and down the stairwell, of this creaky old house they live in. Vents in the floors as big as table tops. Little or no insulation.

When Sandra was a child she always wondered how her mother knew everything that was going on. It wasn't until she had Peter, had her own house, that she discovered how little could be hidden from a mother, or a father, unless they didn't want to know. How houses were complicitous betrayers of confidences.

Sandra slumps back onto her pillows, pulls the covers up to her chin. She opened the window because Karl likes it open, but she can't stand to have cold shoulders. Once her shoulders are chilled, especially across the back of her neck, her whole body becomes cold. She dozes and wakes, drifts to the edge of sleep before being tugged to wakefulness.

When Karl comes to bed the heat from his body spreads, envelops her. She smells him, yeasty breath, fusty hair. She moves closer, brushes her fingertips along his penis. It thickens. She draws herself under the covers, leans her face into his sweet piss-pungent crotch, licks his balls, licks up the length of his now hard cock. She rubs her cheeks, one side, the other, then her tongue, up and down, up and down. The bathroom door slams. Peter is home. Sandra stops. Karl groans.

It used to be Karl who did the exploring. Every part of her, touching it, bringing it alive. He liked to control their sex, draw it out. Or perform furiously fast, front or back or sideways. Whatever, wherever. Then he stopped. He stopped, and never explained why.

Now Karl only responds.

Lately, since she removed her wedding band, Sandra wants to know Karl's body. Needs to know it, every bit. To have it imprinted on her skin, end to end. On her tongue. Inside her.

Lately there is this relief. This sudden lightness. A generosity. Because Sandra knows she is leaving Karl, she can be benevolent. Karl mutely accepts whatever she offers. But it's just a matter of time.

Sandra gets up and puts on her dressing gown.

"Where are you going?" Karl turns onto his stomach; his face is in his pillow. His voice is muffled, hesitant. He could be crying.

"To talk to Peter."

¤

On nights Sandra doesn't hide in her bedroom, she goes for drives. She likes the familiar metal-and-upholstery smell of the car. She likes the motion, the feeling of going somewhere. She drives to different neighbourhoods, ones she's never been to. She parks on streets called Beechwood, Seneca, Fern. Soothing names. Rosewood. Hopewell.

She walks on sidewalks beside mown lawns and looks into houses, watches the lives of strangers being played out within the frames of night-lit windows. She listens to shouts and murmurs, to the sounds of televisions drifting from flickering blue-tinged rooms, to music. Vague sounds, almost indistinguishable. Hypnotic nothing sounds.

Ursula's apartment is cleaner than clean. No dust, nothing living. Off-white walls, beige carpets. There are no pictures of children, or adults, or any living being, but there is a plethora of knick-knacks, and a calendar, which mysteriously disappeared and has yet to be replaced. On the shiny coffee table, a brown vase holds a white plastic flower arrangement.

"Plastic's best," Ursula told her. "Never dies. And I can just dunk it under the tap."

Sometimes as she walks, Sandra compares Ursula's apartment to the houses she sees. Compares Ursula's life, and what could become Sandra's life, to all of this wondrous anonymous possibility: there a blue—a sea-blue—so pretty on that particular wall, defined by a pale yellow trim. Here a garden of white flowers—nicotiana, impatiens, daisies—fragrant and luminous under the moonlight. A light from across the way filtered through a vivid orange mandala, an exotic piece of fabric carelessly tacked across the window. Lives she doesn't know, doesn't care about. Happy or sad, it doesn't matter. It just doesn't matter at all.

Upon arriving home from her drives, Sandra takes Ursula's calendar from the shoebox. With a tiny ruler, which she took from Peter's geometry set, she makes a straight black line, top right to bottom left, across the day that has just passed.

When she enters his bedroom, Peter is sitting on the side of his bed. His long thin feet, so like Karl's, are bare. He's slumped forward, one hand holding his forehead, the fingers of the other hand stroking the top of his foot. Back and forth. Back and forth. He's crying.

"What's wrong?"

Sandra sits beside him, leans over and touches his toes, runs her fingers along them and takes the hand that has been stroking his foot in hers.

"Tell me."

"Everything. You and Dad. Me and Dad. Me. I'm so fucked up."

"No you aren't, darling." She's lying again, her voice sing-songy and soft. "Well, maybe a little."

She's rewarded with one small laugh.

"Peter, hard times end; they get better." She can't seem to stop lying. (He'll hate her for lying, and for leaving him with Karl. She knows this, knew it from the moment she decided she had to leave; just as she knew she would have to leave anyway.)

Sandra leans closer to Peter and begins to massage each of the fingers of his left hand separately. Peter watches her, turns his hand over when she has finished with the fingers, and opens his palm to her.

She massages his love line, his life line, the line for his intellect. She stretches them, warms them, tries to see if she can find forgiveness in them. When she has finished, she holds his palm in her palm, lifts it to her lips and kisses it. She places her son's hand in his lap.

She begins again with his right hand, careful to avoid the reddened area where he held his finger in the flame of his lighter. She places it, too, in his lap.

She stands then and leans to kiss his hair. It is damp and smells warm and pungent.

"Go to bed. We'll talk in the morning."

When Sandra crawls back into bed with Karl, he's asleep. She begins again, touching him, licking him until he's awake. She kisses his neck, his armpits, down his chest and stomach. She flips him over, does his back, his ass, his thighs, spreads his legs, flicks her tongue around his balls.

Sandra turns Karl over again, puts him inside her. Rides him until he comes.

¤

This morning, after the massage was finished and Ursula lay naked on the massage table relaxed and quiet—a not-quite-old woman with colourless hair, bloodless skin, too-long finger-nails, scars—Sandra remembered her mother. When she died. Her naked bruised body overwhelmed with needles and gadgets and tubes. When everything had finally been turned off, the room became so quiet that Sandra wished her mother could be there, alive, to enjoy the reprieve. The breathtaking suddenness of the peace.

Sandra watched the nurse remove the tubes and needles, the bags and boards and all the tape that seemed to have held her mother together, to have bound her to life. As Sandra watched, her mother became the woman Sandra remembered: soft olive skin, arched eyebrows still dark in old age, a pert bow mouth. Whole and perfect.

The nurse pulled the curtain to give Sandra some time alone. Sandra stood beside the bed, touched her mother's hand, worrying a bit of adhesive left on her skin. Then she turned away, found a basin, ran warm water and began.

First a thorough hair wash; more water to rinse. She brushed the fine grey hair into place, then washed her mother's face, into her ears, the creases around her nose, down along the wonderful wattles, slack and grey, on her neck.

Sandra washed her mother's bruised co-operative body, remembered it alive. Washed it tenderly, with reverence and with care. It seemed to her that her mother had not quite gone. Not that she was there with her, but that she was in transition. A changeling. Not herself anymore, but not yet what she would become. The potential for grief was present, its shadings and its nuances, and all its pain and regret, but it was not then manifest.

That's what Sandra feels now as she lies beside Karl. Soon their lives will change. Sandra has made a decision. But for now there is this interval, this place in time without boundaries, without clear allegiances, and, at this particular moment, without remorse.

Karl's hand rests on the sheet.

"You could start talking to Peter," Sandra says. She traces the shape of his hand with her fingertip.

"You're going to leave us, aren't you?" Karl asks.

They lie together, still wet, she tracing his hand, he with his eyes closed.

"Yes, I am."

She looks at his eyelids so thin and blue-veined. So fragile.

"Soon," she says. "But not right now, not right this very minute."

Night Watch: A Quartet

Nimbostratus
November
Anniversary
Night Watch

Nimbostratus

Pamela waits on the platform opposite the bus station. She stands on the edge of the sidewalk, as close to the road as she can be without stepping onto it. Like the weather, she is a stationary front. She'd like to move, if only for warmth, for the bitter air holds the mean still feel of imminent snow.

The sky is low and enveloping. The sad mottled grey of old metal: dull pitted nickels or the faded aging chrome on ailing cars. Occasionally, Pamela notices a ragged bit of blue-black cloud scudding beneath the nimbostratus layer, diffusing, then disappearing. It's 10:47 a.m. Her bus should be here in thirteen minutes. It will leave fifteen minutes after it arrives.

Pamela's nose is red; her ears are frost-bitten and hurting. Her mother told her to wear a hat, but Pamela didn't. Her mother is always telling her things: "Wear a hat." "Don't be out late." "Do up your coat." "Do you have enough money?"

¤

"Well, do you?"

Her mother's voice was thin and sad. Pamela heard the sadness, but didn't look up.

"What?"

"Money. Do you have enough money?"

"I told you when you asked at breakfast. Yes then. Yes now. Yes, I have enough money."

"I say the same thing over and over because you never seem to listen."

They listened together to the final click of the snap on Pamela's suitcase as she pressed it into place.

"I have everything I need."

Pamela's voice was patient, but distant. Already gone. Already on the bus travelling east, first to Toronto, then to Montreal where Pamela knew she'd cry when she thought about herself and Ricky. About two summers ago, and how hot it had been. How that trip was her first outside the boundaries of Ontario.

After Montreal the bus would go to Truro, Nova Scotia, then to North Sydney, Cape Breton. To Chipper. He'd be at the station to pick her up.

"The guy with the long hair," he'd said on the phone, as though she should expect that more than his hair had changed. As though he'd been gone longer than five months and he'd been transformed. "And a beard. I've grown a beard. Ha-ha-ha."

Chipper was always laughing. That's why they called him Chipper.

"I'll be at the station to pick you up," he'd said.

Pamela set the suitcase on the floor. Her mother took a step closer to her and started to reach out, then dropped her hand to her side.

"Did you pack the sweater Cecily gave you? Do you have some Kleenex?"

"Mumma, stop!"

But Pamela turned to her mother and touched her forehead to her mother's chest. Just for an instant. Just long enough to feel the damp from her mother's tears, but not long enough for her mother to respond.

"I'm going now."

She brushed her fingers across the faded yellow chenille bedspread. She picked up her suitcase, and as she slipped past her mother, she called to her sister Cecily to wake their father, it was time to go. She walked through the doorway, left her mother to stand alone in her bedroom, the room between her parents' and Cecily's, that had been Pamela's since the day she was born.

When she turned to sit in the car, she saw her mother at the window. Her mother's eyes peering through a cleared circle of mist, her palm pressed flat against the pane. Red streaks, like blood, showing where a line of condensation had trickled to reveal the red of her mother's slacks through the haze on the steamy glass.

¤

Last night Pamela couldn't sleep. She'd walked to her mother's bed and stood beside it just as she used to when she was a child. Her father worked the night shift, so on weeknights her mother slept alone.

"Mumma?"

Her mother pulled the covers back. Pamela crawled in. But as soon as her head settled on the pillow, she knew she'd made a mistake.

"You OK?" her mother asked and rolled onto her side.

"Yes."

"Then good night."

Her mother reached to touch Pamela, missed, then rolled onto her back. She put her arms under the covers, tucked them straight down at her sides, fingertips just under the edges of her legs, thumbs curled over the tops. Pamela knew without looking, because her mother always slept like that. At least according to her father she did.

"She sleeps like a soldier."

He jerked his thumb in her mother's direction, then lay down on the floor to show Pamela and Cecily exactly how their mother slept.

"Hardly ever moves. She could sleep through a gaw-damn earthquake."

Pamela didn't really want to know this about her mother, about what her father knew about her mother from sleeping with her, but once it had been said, once it was out in the open, it was an image that endured.

¤

Pamela didn't sleep. She lay on her father's side of the bed, hugging the edge of the mattress, afraid she'd disturb her mother. She lay like that all night, listening to her mother sleep:

Her mother breathing in shallow sighs. The sighs deepening. Lengthening. Finally each breath becoming a rhythmic, melancholy snore.

¤

Eight more minutes. The plain-faced clock is on the outside wall across from the platform. The clock is covered by a metal grille, but still the glass beneath it has been smashed.

Pamela can see her father and Cecily huddled together on the bench just inside the automatic doors. Her father reads his paper, sips coffee from a Styrofoam cup. He came home from work early so he could drive her to the station. He didn't trust Cecily to drive, he said. Not since her accident. She'd totalled the car and walked away with just a bruise on her knee. A miracle, the policeman who charged her said. She was going 80 miles an hour in a 30-mile zone.

Pamela knew her father was tired. He hated working nights. But all bread deliveries had to be made before store opening. Salesmen had become little more than truck drivers, her father complained almost every Friday in his after-supper rant.

"They think bread sells itself. They don't want us to be seen. There's no pride left in the industry. We slink in at dawn, unload our wares, restock the shelves and leave without ever seeing or talking to a customer. The store managers think that good fairies just 'magic' the bread onto the shelves. Poof!"

Here her father stands and prances about the room doing his fairy imitation: mincing steps, knees knifing high, arms rising and falling, fingers flicking open and shut into the air. He chants poof-poof-poof with each flick. Then he falls heavily into his La-Z-Boy recliner and boots up the foot rest.

"Poof!"

He flicks his fingers into the air one last time.

"Gaw-damn truck drivers."

The same speech every time, with Pamela and Cecily and their mother mouthing the words and flicking their fingers into the air whenever he turns his back to them, straight-faced when he turns to face them again. Then he falls asleep, head tilted sideways, mouth open, lips flapping slightly as his breathing deepens, the TV tuned to nonsense.

¤

On a normal day Pamela's father comes home from work around 11:30 a.m. and hits the La-Z-Boy. He reads the paper while drinking endless cups of black coffee that never seem to prevent him from falling asleep. He is there crackling his paper when they come home for lunch, but by the time they leave again for school or work, he's dozing.

"Go to bed, Dad."

He jerks his head up, tries to open his eyes. His paper slides off his lap page by page with a quiet sound like dry autumn leaves sifting onto the ground.

"Go to bed."

"I'll go when I'm gaw-damn good and ready!"

She knows, they all know, he hates to go to bed without Pamela's mother. He used to say it out loud, just after he started working nights and was so emotional, weepy, about everything. "I'm tired all the time," he said to explain away the tears. "Just can't seem to get enough sleep in the g-d daytime."

When they come home in the evening they find him still asleep in his chair, paper strewn, coffee cold in the cup. They cover him and leave him be.

This morning, because she was leaving, he came home early, said he'd go back and finish his route after he saw Pamela off at the bus station. "Too bad what the g-d managers think. Too bad if they have to actually see me in the store." He paced in front of the picture window.

"Sit down, Dad." Pamela looked out the window. She watched her father's reflection move back and forth. "I think it's going to snow," she said.

He walked past her, turned and came back again. "If I sit, I'll fall asleep." Back and forth. "And I want to drive you to the station."

"Please sit down."

"I don't trust Cecily to drive, not since the accident." Then he stopped pacing. "Chipper's a good boy."

Pamela spun around to face him. He squinted his eyes as if the sun was shining into them.

"I'm going out for a cigarette," he said.

He was always doing that, changing the subject before it could become one, before Pamela could argue with him.

Pamela had tried to tell her father that there was nothing between herself and Chipper. They were just friends.

She'd tried to explain to him about Ricky, how she might still love him. How he'd been set up. That the marijuana the police found in his apartment had been planted there by some thugs sent by his Montreal suppliers, who thought Ricky was trying to rip them off. He hadn't paid the money he owed them, that was true. He was going to pay them. But the market was slow. And the cops were more vigilant. It was harder to sell on the street.

She tried to tell him that Ricky never dealt pot or hard drugs, only hashish. He was a hash connoisseur; grass was beneath him, hard drugs were for losers. But her father wouldn't listen. He put his hands over his ears and told her she better shut up, none of this made any difference as far as he was concerned. Ricky was a gaw-damn criminal and that was that.

She shouted that she wanted to go to Ricky's trial and tell the judge about the set-up, but her father wouldn't let her. He told her she had better stay out of it, now and forever, or she'd end up in jail like her boyfriend. And if she did go, he'd kick her out of the house and never let her talk to her mother again.

Pamela had continued to argue with her father about going to the trial, but in the end Ricky had called and told her not to come. He was breaking up with her. He said it wasn't because he might go to jail, because he was sure he'd get off. It was that she'd become a drag; she was always crying (which was true but unfair, considering all she'd been through). He was going back with Brenda, the waitress at the Walper he'd dated before Pamela.

Ricky had told Pamela how shocked he'd been the first time he slept with Brenda and he'd noticed silky black hairs growing around the edge of her almost black nipples. And how a line of the same kind of hair went from her navel to her pubic bush. How he didn't like the hairs at first, but later he did. Pamela's nipples, a pale mauve, and her belly are hairless.

Pamela didn't go to the trial, but she thought she might still love Ricky. Maybe. She wasn't sure. She wasn't sure about anything anymore, except that she needed to be as far away from home as possible. It wasn't that she didn't love her parents and Cecily, but she couldn't stand to be around them, couldn't stand knowing so much about them: that they liked to eat ketchup on their eggs, but didn't like margarine, it was so low-class, they said.

She couldn't stand knowing when Cecily and her mother had their periods, their bloody pads and little bullets of cotton batting wrapped in toilet paper.

Or what cigarettes they smoked and when: Cecily, anything anyone was smoking, any time she could scrounge one, she never bought her own; her father, Players Plain, his first one in the bathroom while he had a bowel movement, which he had like clockwork as soon as he woke up. (Her father said that was the worst thing about shift work. His bowels became used to waking up in the middle of the night. On weekends, when he came back to real time in the real world, his bowels were still on a nighttime schedule.) Her mother, Kools, which she didn't smoke until after supper, then only six, never more, never less.

How her mother held her arms at her sides when she slept, and how her father didn't really sleep at all. She wanted something new, somewhere else. Anywhere else.

Her stomach was always in knots; her skin felt alien and too tight. Rashes appeared on her hands and feet. She could no longer concentrate. She began to sleep as much as possible, taking naps as soon as she arrived home from work, getting up to eat supper, lying down until it was time to go out with her friends. Her mother took her to the doctor for a physical, but all the tests came back normal.

"See. I told you I was fine."

"I needed to know," her mother said.

¤

Pamela watched her father pick up his cigarettes from the table. From the back of the chair he grabbed his uniform jacket, which had "DONNY" emblazoned in gold letters on a bar over his pocket. Pamela wondered why he needed his name there for all the world to see, if nobody ever saw it. He headed for the door. When he reached it he turned to face her.

He took out his cigarettes, put one in his mouth and looked directly at Pamela, scrutinized her for a full minute, his eyes giving up nothing.

"Write your mother," he said.

He went outside and sat on the front step, smoking, until Pamela's mother told him to come inside before he caught his death. He fell asleep in his La-Z-Boy until Pamela had finished packing, and called to Cecily to wake him, it was time to leave.

Now Cecily slouches against her father on the bench in the bus station and smokes his Players Plains, one after another. When she finishes a cigarette, she shifts her body slightly and stretches her leg. With her foot, she triggers the sensor that makes the automatic doors swing open. She flicks her still-lit cigarette butt out the door. Pamela watches the sparks as they bounce along the sidewalk. Then Cecily takes another cigarette from her father's pack and lights it.

The cold air rushes into the station and presses against their father's newspaper. He struggles to gain control of it, turns and glares at Cecily, mouths words Pamela can't hear. Cecily doesn't even look at him, blows smoke straight out, stares ahead. Then he shakes the paper to straighten it and takes another sip of his coffee.

Pamela's feet are fully numb, past pain. They will hurt later, when they thaw on the bus. And the damp penetrates her new navy blue wool pea jacket and makes her shoulders ache. But she doesn't even shrug. Her need to leave has riveted her in place, as though, if she moves, if she takes her eyes from the grey horizon where the headlights of the bus will appear—if she even blinks—the bus will never come.

Beside her on the sidewalk are her suitcases. One suitcase is big, modern and plastic, the same grey as the winter sky. She'd bought it at the Sally Ann last week, when she decided, on the spur of the moment, to take Chipper up on his offer of a place to stay. Maybe you'll fall in love with me, he'd said when Pamela called to make arrangements for him to pick her up in Cape Breton, but he'd been saying that forever.

"I can help you forget Ricky. He's locked up. And he's in love with Brenda." Chipper paused to let this sink in. "Maybe you'll fall in love with me." He'd laughed—ha-ha-ha—as though he didn't really mean it.

"Maybe I won't," she'd told Chipper, "but I'll see you next week."

"Maybe's good enough for me." Then he'd laughed again.

The big grey case holds nothing important. Things her mother packed for her: a dress ("Just in case," she said as she folded it in tissue paper). A skirt and blouse ("You'll be applying for jobs, won't you?" she asked, but it wasn't really a question). Pantyhose. Two boxes of Kotex. A sewing kit with three buttons, and thread in four basic colours: black, white, blue and brown. A card of safety pins.

The other suitcase is a musty square tan-coloured box with expandable hinges that she'd "borrowed" from her parents two years ago to take to Montreal the first time she went with Ricky to score hashish. It had been July. Hot and muggy. She'd never taken the suitcase out of the trunk of the car. Not to brush her teeth, or change her sweaty top, or after she and Ricky made love and her panties became streaked with semen and blood.

She'd been at the end of her period. The safest time, Ricky said, as he nuzzled her, licked her sweaty belly, the insides of her thighs, the backs of her hands, her wrists, each licked-wet place becoming cooler until it dried.

She'd liked the feel of the wet between her legs as they walked down Saint Catherine Street on their way to drink *bière froide* and eat *patates frites*.

¤

The tan case holds everything she needs: five pairs of underwear; a bra; some long johns. A big violent-pink plastic cosmetic case stuffed with toiletries and some cheap jewellery; the cherry red Ingo sweater from Cecily that her mother'd asked her about; an extra pair of jeans; her sneakers; three T-shirts; some socks of various colours and thicknesses. The once-white handkerchief crusted with dried blood that she'd double-wrapped in a bread bag and was all she had left of Ricky since he broke up with her and landed in jail.

Her relic, she'd told Chipper when she showed it to him while they waited for their beer at the Walper, a week before Chipper had left for Cape Breton. They'd gone to check out Brenda, to see how she measured up. Pamela'd told Chipper about the hair on Brenda's breasts and belly.

Brenda set the beer on the table and left.

"Too much make-up, not enough ass and hairy tits."

Chipper hadn't even tried to be quiet.

Brenda pivoted, looked just past their shoulders, then turned and walked away.

Pamela told Chipper she'd never give up the handkerchief, not even if she fell in love with him the way he always wanted her to.

"It's my relic."

She showed it to him, dry rusty powder sifting onto her hands. She'd already told Chipper what it was like to walk into Ricky's apartment building and ring his number. She knew he was home because he'd called her and asked her to come by after she finished work. She stood in the lobby pressing 304. Waited for the buzz that would let her in. 304. 304.

While she waited, something dripped onto her hair. She reached up and brushed at it. Water, she thought, rubbing her hand on her jeans.

She continued pressing: 304! 304! 304! 304! More drips fell onto her hair. Then onto her neck. She brushed at them again, moved out of the way. She looked up. She looked down at her hand. Looked up again. That's when she started to scream.

Ricky was up there, tied to the chandelier, his once shiny brown eyes hidden inside lacerated pulpy puffs of meaty red flesh, his lips split and drooling blood, his nose a mangled displaced wad of skin with white bone showing through. This bleeding mask dangled, bobbed, while the rest of Ricky's body had been stretched and curved around the light fixture, belly down, legs pulled back and strung to the base of the chandelier, his arms pulled up to meet his feet.

When the police and ambulance attendants finally lifted Ricky down, Pamela rushed over with the handkerchief a policeman had given her to wipe her hands and neck. She dabbed at the blood on Ricky's face until the attendant pulled her away. That's when Ricky was busted, when the police checked his apartment after the ambulance had taken him to the hospital.

"My souvenir of Ricky."

She'd held the handkerchief out for Chipper to see, then rolled it into a ball and put it back into the bread bag where she kept it.

Oh, and she had a piece of hash the size of a large brownie, and the same colour, tucked inside her cosmetic case. It was from Ricky, too. Money in the bank, he said when he'd given it to her.

"It's money in the bank, Pammy."

They were at the truck stop where they'd pulled off Highway 401 on their way home from their third buying trip in Montreal. Ricky wanted to smoke up, and he wanted Pamela to test the merchandise with him. (Ricky was the only person she allowed to call her Pammy. Pammy was the other thing, besides Ricky, she was leaving behind forever. And it felt exactly right. Good-bye Ricky, and good-bye Pammy. Sayonara. Good riddance.)

Ricky had already tested the hash with Jean-Marie, the fidgety bearded leprechaun who had sold him the dope. Now he was cutting two slabs from one of the bricks, thick slices.

"This one's for your personal use."

Ricky wrapped the hash in plastic wrap and laid it in her hand with the solemnity of a priest imparting the host.

The park behind the truck stop was dusty and deserted. They sat on top of a grubby carved-up once-red picnic table. Wasps buzzed around spills and sticky patches, around their eyes and lips. Truck gears rumbled up or down depending on which way the truckers were headed, in or out. Air brakes hissed into the heat.

"And this is for a rainy day."

He'd handed her the second slab, and they'd laughed and laughed because the sun was as bright as a new penny in a sky that was limitless and blue. Because this was their life, and they imagined it would always be the way it was now. And they laughed because the dope was exceptionally good.

"Ex-cep-tion-al-ly fucking go-od!"

Ricky laughed harder and kissed Pamela on the lips, and Pamela tasted tobacco and the thick resiny oil of the drug on his tongue.

¤

The sky darkens. It feels as if night is approaching, though it's 10:57 a.m. An oily metallic smell rises from the frozen asphalt and does not dissipate. There is no wind.

Pamela hadn't needed to use the "rainy day" slab, so she wrapped it inside a sanitary napkin and tucked it into her pink cosmetic case. Ready if she ever does need it. She still has a small piece of the personal-use hash, too, wrapped in foil in her cigarette pack. In case she wants a toke, which she will, before she meets Chipper in Cape Breton.

Chipper is Ricky's best friend. He's Pamela's best friend, too, next to Cecily, then Ricky before he went to jail and broke up with her, then her high school girlfriend, Suzi Bauer, who is in Toronto at Teachers' College. Pamela really misses her. Suzi says she'll write Pamela in Cape Breton and come to visit in the summer if Pamela has a place where she can stay. Suzi is going to meet Pamela's bus in Toronto, and they'll have a coffee and a cigarette, maybe a toke in the washroom, while they wait for Pamela's connection to Montreal.

Pamela watches the bus turn the corner and drive slowly toward her. Where there has been little sound except for the occasional swish as the automatic doors to the station open, there is now noise everywhere: the hiss of brakes, the thunk of cold plastic hitting even colder concrete, coughing, noses being blown. People have been coming out of the station and lining up their suitcases beside Pamela's for the last few minutes, but no one has spoken. Now everyone needs to talk.

Pamela can still see her father, watches him look up, then fold his paper and set it on the bench. Cecily is already moving toward the door. Then the bus is in front of her. The bus door opens and a whoosh of warm air envelops Pamela for a moment. The driver descends, closes the door from the outside and moves through the crowd to lift up the doors to the baggage compartments. He takes Pamela's suitcases and shoves them inside.

Cecily and her father are beside her now, Cecily hugging her, saying she's going to come visit in the summer if their parents will let her. If she can save enough money from her part-time job. Her father stands to the side, then steps forward and takes her arm. He jiggles it slightly, squeezes it, then hands her a Mars bar, some Chiclets, a pack of Rothmans and a teen magazine, the kind Pamela hasn't read for years. She reaches with her free arm and grabs her father around the neck, pulls him down to her and tries to kiss him on the cheek, but misses and hits somewhere near his ear.

The driver comes back to the front of the line and opens the door. And Pamela walks up the steps, gives up the first portion of her ticket, stuffs her pea jacket into the overhead compartment, settles herself into her seat beside the window.

Her father and Cecily are holding hands. They wave with their free hands. Pamela waves back and then leans forward and presses her face to the glass, distorting her lips and nose. She watches them laugh. The bus rumbles. People push by. A woman her mother's age sits beside her and immediately starts to read. Blasts of warm air mix with cold, and then the door hisses shut and there is one last cold blast. Finally, only warm air circulates.

Pamela checks the window again. Her father and Cecily have their hands in their pockets. They take them out to wave. Pamela waves back. Blows kisses. Cecily blows kisses with both her hands. Her father waves one last time and turns away. Pamela waves. Cecily turns.

Pamela watches them walk away. She rises, moves past the woman beside her. She walks up the aisle to the driver, who is counting tickets.

"Is it still possible to change my ticket? I want to go to Vancouver."

"Where are you supposed to go?"

"Cape Breton."

"That's quite a change. You can make it in Toronto."

He tells her that there might be a processing fee, and she'll have to pay the difference in the fares.

Pamela returns to her place, squeezes past the reading woman again, looks out the window, but her father and her sister are gone. There is a hiss as the brakes are released, and the bus moves forward.

As she leans back into her seat, Pamela sees the first flakes of snow begin to fall. Leisurely, as if they might change their minds and return again to the clouds. The nimbostratus layer thickens; the sky darkens. Snow begins to swirl past her window. A disorderly profusion of fat flakes, feathery white crystals of ice, lacy and soft. They dance up on the wind, are held on some imperceptible current, rise further into the air, turn, and turn again. Then silently, slowly, they begin their gentle irrevocable descent.

November

While Cecily was dying, Pamela perfected her pie crust. Each day she tried something new. A little more salt. Half lard, half shortening. Melted ice cubes instead of cold water from the tap. Three tablespoons of butter, a pinch of nutmeg and a teaspoon of brown sugar.

The day Cecily became too weak to talk and began to slip in and out of sleep—more in than out, though no one suggested this sleeping might be a coma—Pamela made an apple pie. She peeled, then sliced spy apples wafer-thin. Layer upon layer of them, their pale yellow flesh oozing onto her spiced and buttery pie crust. She poured a mixture of sour cream, brown sugar, cinnamon, ground walnuts and flour over the top of the pie, dotted it with butter, then went to the hospice and held Cecily's hand, tracing with her floury fingers a browning bruise on the underside of her sleeping sister's wrist.

It had been a kind fall. Long and hopeful, days and days of sunshine. Sometimes Pamela pushed Cecily down the hospice corridor to one of the big windows that overlooked the courtyard. They seldom talked, Pamela because she seemed to have too much to say as Cecily had less and less.

Pamela brushed Cecily's hair, Cecily's head bobbing back and forth with each stroke, her eyes closed.

"That's nice," she might say, if she spoke at all.

Sometimes Cecily said, "Go home, Pamela. You make me tired."

Pamela had stopped protesting, stopped telling Cecily that she only wanted her to get well. When she did try to tell her, Cecily closed her eyes, turned away from her.

"See," she said. "Please go."

Pamela went home and made pie crust. Refrigerate all ingredients for one hour, the recipe said. Use one egg and one teaspoon of vinegar to five cups of flour.

Lines and lines of noisy geese streamed south in scattered Vs that disintegrated, then reformed. Cecily never heard them.

"Did you hear the geese this morning? They were so loud."

"No I didn't," Cecily said. Or she might just shake her head.

At home, Pamela's neighbours stood on their porches. They watched the geese, waved to Pamela and exclaimed, "Quite a sight." Or, "More this year than ever." Or, "It's gonna be a cold winter."

The smell of baking pie drifted from Pamela's door across her porch. Across theirs.

"What kind today?" they'd ask, for one or the other of them would be eating some of this pie for supper.

"Apple. Spy apple."

Pamela cut a slice for her husband Brian, one for her son Martin, and one for Cecily, which she placed on her Limoges china—a gift from Brian's mother in Vancouver. The same routine every day.

Cecily's pie was always gone the next morning, the plate washed and wrapped in a plastic bag. Cecily could only eat blueberry jam mixed with yoghurt, or ice cream and maple syrup. Sometimes baby food: strained carrots, puréed pears, minced chicken. Three or four spoonfuls at most. Her mouth was filled with sores.

The rest of the pie went to a neighbour. "How is your sister?" they'd ask and shake their heads. "How is she doing today?"

On Hallowe'en night a fierce north wind opened the leaf-protected world to scrutiny. Pamela thought it was exactly the kind of weather it should be. Cecily is dying and it should rain. It should be cold. There should be no comfort in the sky, or the air, or the ground.

The next morning, All Souls' Day, was the day Cecily took up sleeping, the day Pamela baked the spy apple pie.

¤

Cecily Winifred Hauck was born on November 3, the feast day of St. Winifred. St. Winifred's uncle became a saint before she did: St. Beuno. Cecily could have been a saint. She was odd and obsessive, and one year left the ashes from Ash Wednesday on her forehead for two weeks, placing a piece of clear tape over the black smudge. She refused to wash her forehead, a perfect rectangle of grime forming along the edges of the tape.

Their mother finally removed the tape and Cecily's ashes during the night. Pamela knew because she saw her mother slink down the hallway in the dark, sneak into Cecily's room, then sneak out. The next morning Cecily wailed when she felt her forehead where the tape and ashes should have been. Their mother, who was pouring juice for breakfast, just rolled her eyes.

Pamela never wanted to be a saint, not even when she was at her most fervent in Grade Five, in Sister Emily's class. She cleaned blackboards after school for Indulgences, went to Mass every day in Lent and Advent and filled mission cards with dimes. She gave her only doll, one with green hair that was a twin to Cecily's, which had blue hair, to the Poor Children in Bolivia.

In Grade Six Pamela tried Suzi Bauer's lipstick and eyeshadow at recess just after school started in September. Suzi Bauer made a heart over the "i" in her name. She was the first girl to wear nylons to school. She was tall and thin but had breasts, and her periods had already started.

Sister Aloysius gave Pamela the strap. "Good girls don't wear make-up," she said as she whacked Pamela's hands, five on the left, five on the right. Pamela didn't cry. "You're a sinful girl, Pamela Hauck, and so is that Suzi Bauer," Sister said, which is exactly why Pamela became Suzi's best friend. "You must show remorse to be forgiven your wickedness."

Pamela and Cecily's dolls were, of course, called Greeny and Bluey. Pamela was never given another one. Cecily graduated to Barbies. Sometimes Pamela would have liked to play Barbies, too.

Around 650 BC, Winifred was beheaded by Caradoc because she turned away his sexual advances. St. Beuno retrieved his niece's head from the ground and, being a saint, restored it to Winifred's body, healing her wounds. Pamela wondered how he did this. Did he place the head back on Winifred's shoulders, then sew the skin together? Did he trace the line of the wound with his fingertips? Did he kiss it better?

At the place where Winifred's head had fallen, a spring sprang forth, so Winifred became a saint like her uncle. The spring was called Holywell, or St. Winifred's Well. It became a place of pilgrimage where cures were still reported. After Cecily's cancer spread to her bones, Pamela suggested they go to Wales, to Holywell, to test the cure theory. To try for a miracle.

"Poor Pamela," Cecily said.

Winifred was also known as Gwenfrewi.

¤

On the day Cecily was born, their mother, while walking with Pamela to Mr. Ruetz's store for cocoa to make hot chocolate, bent over and groaned, then waddled to the Schlueters' porch and sat on the steps.

"Ring the bell, Pamela. Ring Mrs. Schlueter's bell."

"Get up, Mumma."

"Ring the bell."

"You said we'd go to the store."

Pamela turned away.

"Pamela."

Pamela walked to the store. She didn't look back when her mother called. She didn't look back when Mrs. Schlueter called. She knew the way; she'd go alone.

"Can I help you, Pamela?"

Mr. Ruetz followed her as she walked the aisles.

"Mumma said it's cold. She said she'd make hot chocolate. She needs cocoa."

"Where is your mother?"

"At home. She sent me. I'm almost three."

Mr. Ruetz handed her a yellow tin of Fry's Cocoa, but before Pamela reached the door, Mr. Schlueter came through it and grabbed her hand.

"Come now, missy."

Pamela dropped the cocoa.

Mr. Schlueter took her home. He sat in her father's chair reading her father's newspaper. Pamela sat on the edge of her bed. When her father came home he sat beside her and told her she had a baby sister.

"Mr. Schlueter sat in your chair."

"The baby's name is Cecily Winifred."

"I want Mumma."

"She'll be home in a week."

Pamela thought her mother stayed away because Pamela had been bad. She thought it was her fault her mother was in the hospital. And because she was bad, her father sent her to stay with her aunt and uncle and her two cousins. She wanted to stay at home with her father, but he said, "No, it's all arranged. You're staying at your cousins. You'll have someone to play with."

Pamela didn't play with her cousins, whose house smelled like bacon fat and onions. Pamela looked at books and walked to the picture window, pressed her hands and cheeks against the glass, waited for her father's evening visit. He came at supper time, stayed for half an hour, then left to visit her mother in the hospital.

Her cousins slept in single beds. Pamela had a cot in their room, but she never slept. After her bath her uncle dried her. She refused to look at him, refused to answer his questions about her day or the new baby she'd never seen and never wanted to see. He helped her into her pyjamas, then tucked her into bed. She didn't like it when his skin touched hers. She tried to hold her skin away from his.

Her cousins had bulging eyes and their lids never fully closed over them. Pamela couldn't tell if they were asleep or awake. She was so frightened of their open eyes she tried to stay awake, in case they wanted to do something terrible to her. But the most terrible thing was their half-open eyes.

On one visit her father brought her a Turkish Delight, his favourite. Pamela refused to share it with him, even when he asked. She held it tightly in her fist, the paper crinkling and crackling.

She didn't share it with her cousins, though she hated Turkish Delight. She flushed it down the toilet. She flushed the toilet five times because at first the chocolate bar floated. When the wrapper came off the bar sank. The bar didn't go down, but the wrapper did, and the water rose to the top of the toilet. The fifth time the chocolate bar disappeared and the water only came to the regular level.

On the seventh day her father came for her in the car. Pamela didn't say good-bye, didn't wave as they backed out the driveway. Her cousins and her aunt and uncle stood at the picture window and waved and waved, but Pamela remained steadfast. When she arrived home she refused to speak to her mother, who helped her take off her coat and hat. When her mother sat on the sofa and put her breast in the baby's mouth, Pamela stood in front of her and stared.

Pamela had never seen such a thing, a hairless pink blob all mouth and waving fists, latched onto her mother's breast. The blob was pulling at her mother's breast and her mother let it.

Pamela's fists were balled tightly at her sides. She watched. Then in one fast move she reached out. With one hand she pinched the baby's cheek, with the other hand she pinched her mother's breast. Hard. As hard as she could. Harder still. Then she let go.

The baby screamed. Her mother screamed. Milk flew from the breast. Pamela screamed. She thought she had made her mother bleed. Her mother slapped her on the cheek.

"Go to your room!"

For three days Pamela could see, though only faintly, the impression of her mother's fingers on her skin.

During their childhood together Pamela would wound her sister physically and dramatically two more times. But after the first three days of living with a sister had passed, and the blush of her mother's slap had almost disappeared, Pamela called a truce. She steered clear of the baby. And her mother began to spend some time with her away from Cecily.

¤

Cecily was tall. Five-ten. Almost as tall as their father. Pamela was five-four, and their mother five-two. As she lay dying Cecily seemed diminished, less herself and more like them. Pamela could see in her their father's nubby cheekbones, their mother's weak chin, and the same tired dowdiness Pamela was acquiring as she neared middle age.

Cecily had never been dowdy. Even as a child she liked to layer her clothes. Two pairs of socks: one pair knee socks, one pair ankle socks, different colours. Crinolines, slips, felt poodle skirts from the dress-up box, a long-sleeved shirt with a short-sleeved one over it, different colours. The brighter the better.

She never wore a coat, but wore layers of sweaters, scarves wrapped around her neck, ridiculous toques. She had frizzy wheat-coloured hair, almost invisible eyebrows and lashes, eyes the same purple as irises. Her skin smelled like peaches when she washed, like fermenting fruit when she didn't.

She was single.

In the spring, when Cecily learned that her cancer had spread, she ranted, "I'm glad I never married, glad I don't have some man's name instead of my own. I'd change my name back to Hauck if I were you, Pamela. Why did you change your name in the first place? We were born Haucks. We should die Haucks."

She ordered Pamela to make real coffee, to make it strong. (She'd been drinking organic vegetable juices she made herself, taking vitamins in large doses, using royal bee jelly.) She bought six Laura Secord French Mint Chocolate bars after she left the doctor's office with the bad news, and she intended to eat every one. She wanted lots of hot milk and white sugar in her coffee. (She'd given up all dairy products and all refined sugars.)

"Hauck will be on my grave," she shouted to Pamela who was in the kitchen making coffee. "On my grave. Do you hear me? And stop crying, Pamela. Stop it!"

Pamela didn't stop crying while she made the coffee. She continued to cry while she served it. She cried, though silently, while she ate the chocolate Cecily gave her.

¤

The ways in which Pamela wounded Cecily were really both the same. She broke her sister's collarbone. Twice. Once when Cecily was standing beside her on their stained green sectional sofa. Cecily's fleshy legs straddled two sections. Pamela sat beside her, watched Cecily from the corner of her eye.

Pamela turned. She placed her feet on the other side of the divide and shoved the sections—ever so gently, ever so slowly—apart. She chattered to Cecily until Cecily thumped like an onion on to the floor.

Cecily didn't cry. At first. Then she screamed and screamed. Their mother arrived. Pamela stood in the doorway saying, "She fell, Mumma. She fell."

Her mother didn't hear her. She scooped Cecily off the floor and yelled for their father. He came, and they left in the car. Left Pamela alone in the house. Pamela pushed the sofa back together. (It took some effort.) She sat on the edge of the seat and waited. Mrs. Schlueter arrived and told her Cecily had a broken collarbone, and Pamela was to come to Mrs. Schlueter's house to wait until her family arrived home.

When the car drove into the driveway, Pamela went to the Schlueter's door. She watched as her father lifted Cecily, her bare chest and shoulders wrapped in layer upon layer of beige tensor bandage, from the car. He carried her like a princess into the house. Pamela followed behind. He placed Cecily in bed, covered her. He told Pamela to leave Cecily alone, she needed to sleep.

Cecily was allergic to tensor bandages. No one knew until her armpits swelled and the skin along the edges of the cloth split like dropped melons. After Cecily healed, her scars became thick ridges of sensitive pink skin which wrapped round and round itself.

¤

The second time she broke Cecily's collarbone was an accident. They were playing Statues. It was Pamela's turn to twirl.

"Faster," Cecily yelled. "Faster."

Pamela twirled Cecily faster. And faster.

"More."

And Pamela went faster still. As fast as she could. Then she let go of Cecily.

Cecily flew and flew. She landed. Contorted. At first she laughed, then she didn't. She looked at Pamela, her face turning whiter and whiter. And Pamela knew. Then Cecily knew. It was there in her eyes. And she screamed, louder than the first time.

¤

The day before Cecily died, Pamela helped a nurse lift her sister higher in bed. They freshened her pillows, changed the cover on the top one. As they eased Cecily back onto the bed, her gown slipped away from her thin shoulders. There were the scars. Now white, still thick and fibrous. They wrapped under Cecily's armpits like botched seams on a sleeve.

"Keloid," the nurse said, and she touched one with her fingertips.

"I know."

Pamela wanted to touch them, too. With her fingertips, with her lips. She wanted to lick the scars until they dissolved. She knew then they would always be on her sister's body. It might have been the worst thing she'd ever done. Hurting Cecily, scarring her like that.

"She's very ill," the nurse said.

Because Cecily was dying, Pamela stayed with her overnight. Wiped her forehead, talked to her about the change in the weather.

"The leaves are gone. It's rained every day since Hallowe'en. Yesterday there were even a few snowflakes. I hope the geese are in Miami. Mumma and Dad are coming. I called them. I made lemon meringue pie. I squeezed fresh lemons. The pie crust is Mumma's recipe. I think I have it perfected now."

The lemon pie, its flaky crust as white as the meringue, and just as delicate, sat on the Limoges plate; a cloth napkin the colour of pumpkin sat beside it. On the napkin was a silver fork. Pamela had arranged these things on the metal dresser beside Cecily's bed.

Around 10 p.m. Pamela left to find a coffee. When she returned a man in coveralls, who had a moon face, round eyes and almost pouty lips, sat in her chair. He was eating lemon pie, and between mouthfuls, told Cecily about some of the people in the hospice. About Janice Blair in room 210 who was actually being sent home because she wouldn't die. She seemed to be getting better. How it was a wonderful jest which made everyone hopeful.

Pamela stood in the doorway listening. She stepped into the room.

"That's not your pie."

She sounded vicious even to herself.

"Put it down. It's Cecily's pie."

She strode toward the man and grabbed the plate from his hand. The pie slide onto the floor.

"Get out. You can't have the pie. Can't you see she needs it?"

The man stood. He lifted his hands, palms up.

"She said I could eat it."

Pamela didn't care.

"When? When did she tell you? Look at her. She can't talk. How could she tell you to eat her pie?"

The man put his thin hands in the air, in surrender, shook his head and walked out of the room.

Pamela knew Cecily gave the pie away, she just didn't want to know. She wanted Cecily to eat the pie. Most of all, Pamela wanted to think Cecily ate it. She needed the illusion of Cecily sitting up every night, eating, laughing because she was fooling them all, tricking them into thinking she was too sick to eat her favourite food. Washing the plate, wrapping it neatly in a plastic bag. That's all Pamela really wanted. Some impossible morsel of hope in the face of the crushing certainty of Cecily's death.

Cecily died at ten o'clock the next morning. She was thirty-three years and three days old. The rain stopped and the sun came out, but the air remained bitter.

After she helped her parents make arrangements for Cecily, Pamela went home. She took out flour and shortening. Butter and salt. She melted an ice cube in a teacup. She made *pets de soeurs*. Pie crust sprinkled with a mixture of butter, brown sugar, flour and cinnamon, rolled into a pinwheel, then sliced and baked on a cookie sheet. Comfort food, Cecily called them when their mother made them with her leftover pastry.

When they cooled Pamela placed a dozen on a Limoges plate and covered the plate with plastic wrap. She wrote a note. She drove to the hospice. She asked the desk attendant to give the *pets de soeurs* to the moon-faced janitor.

"Victor," the attendant said.

"Yes, Victor."

"He's good with the guests."

Pamela wanted to say that there were no guests in a hospice. Instead she nodded.

"I suppose he is."

The note said everything Pamela had ever wanted to say. It said: I'm sorry.

Anniversary

The second time in their marriage that Pamela stopped wanting to have sex with Brian came after her sister Cecily died. Occasionally she let Brian get on top of her and bounce around, but she felt lonely afterwards. And she couldn't sleep. Once Brian had finished she got up and washed between her legs, then wandered through her darkened house, stopped and looked out of frosted windows, pressed her face there. Her forehead, her cheeks, her lips.

The snow, a restful glittering pillow, muffled noise, gentled it. All soothing phwoosh-phwooshes, like the sound velvet would make if it were a sound. If she had had the energy she would have gone out into the snow, laid down in it, waited for the promised calm of the dreams of those who die of the cold.

"You dominate our sex. I don't get a chance to understand what I want," she told Brian when he said that having sex with her—when it happened at all—was like necrophilia. He attempted a laugh, an uneasy heh-heh-heh.

"I'm trying to be patient," he said. It came out sounding like a whine.

"You always initiate and you expect me to respond. If I don't respond, what will happen? 'What will he do?' I ask myself," she said. "So when I think I have to, I give in. Because I'm afraid to say no all of the time."

She didn't add, "But I'd like to." Instead she asked, "Should I be afraid, Brian?"

"Sex must be boring for you," he said.

Pamela knew he meant that he felt he must be boring her. That he was boring. And he was hurt. Bewildered. But her sadness was so complete it left no room for kindness. The fact remained: she didn't want to have sex.

"Boring isn't the word I'd use," she said.

"What word would you use?" Brian asked, the whine turned to anger.

"I don't know," she told him.

Pamela didn't know what word she wanted to use, but the substance of the word she was trying to find had nothing to do with sex. It had to do with stillness. It had to do with cessation. Of sound, of smell, of touch, and of both need and desire. She wanted to look at the world as it existed without Cecily. To see, in the same way that she felt it, the vacancy Cecily's death had left. She wanted the ordinary and the daily to stop: dental appointments, meals, sex, laundry, runny noses and fevers, Christmas.

She wanted to think about her imperfect friendship with her sister and what it meant that Pamela had failed Cecily while she was dying. That she'd spent her time baking pies that Cecily couldn't eat. But she didn't know how to say this to Brian.

He would call her at work and say, "You never have time for me." And he was right.

That was a long time ago.

¤

Pamela used to think she must have been a migratory bird in another life. Getting antsy down south, all that sun. Feasting on gigantic Florida cockroaches, or oranges and grapefruit left to rot on trees. Too abundant suddenly. Then some instinctual urge for less, for a test: a long flight, a freak blizzard over Cape Cod, sparse grass, few insects or seeds, and no choice but to mate and spend every bit of daylight scrounging for food to sustain young.

A pull to the north. Or anywhere.

Yes that's how she used to feel every spring: anxious for change, for movement, for sex, raw and primal. Maybe she still feels that way but just doesn't let it in. The life Pamela lives now is cautious and set. Celibate. She hadn't seen that coming.

Brian left her. For Suzi. Silly name. Fifties all the way. Suzi Parker. Suzi-Q. Wake Up, Little Suzi. Dotting the "i" with a heart when she was young. Pamela hadn't taken the woman named Suzi seriously. At least not as Brian's lover. Maybe because Suzi had been Pamela's best friend. Their friend.

Brian told her about Suzi the day he and Pamela were supposed to leave for Niagara Falls. It was May. Pamela liked travelling in May; it satisfied her cyclical spring anxiety. The Falls had been her idea. Brian always said he wanted to go to the Honeymoon Capital of the World. He said he'd never been there. He felt historically deprived.

She'd planned the trip to make up to Brian. They'd leave Martin with Suzi and Gary. Suzi's son Gary was Martin's best friend. Pamela thought she and Brian should have some time alone together. She'd finished going through the third period when sex with Brian had lost its appeal. It had nothing to do with Brian. Pamela had been feeling middle-aged and sexless: greying hair, thickening body, loosening skin, the odd hot flash. Sometimes her vagina was so dry that when Brian entered her she winced and pushed him out again. If she let him remain inside her, let him finish, afterwards she was raw and sore. Sometimes she bled.

And there seemed to be so little privacy. Martin was older and seemed to be around all the time. He stayed up late and they never knew when he might barge in on them. All of a sudden he seemed to take up all of the space in the house with his long body, his enormous feet, his loud music, his smells, his constant entourage of friends, his appetite. Pamela had become a bit shy of him, and of Brian. She felt overwhelmed by their maleness.

"Not again," Brian had sighed one night when she said she really didn't want to have sex. They hadn't had sex in five weeks.

"Oh, go ahead then," Pamela had hissed. She stood up on the mattress, yanked off her nightgown and threw it on the floor. She flopped naked onto the bed, faced Brian, watched him, her breasts crushed to her chest with one arm, leaning back on the elbow of the other, her legs splayed, the lips of her vulva gaping.

"What? Am I supposed to be grateful for that?" Brian shoved the covers to the end of the bed.

"Where are you going?" Pamela asked. She tried not to shout it.

"For a walk. For a long, cold walk," he said as he dressed. He slammed the bedroom door.

"Where are you going?" she heard Martin ask him. Martin must have been... Where? Downstairs? In the bathroom? Listening at their door?

"Out," Brian shouted and left.

Brian began walking every night. Sometimes he came to bed smelling like spun sugar or coffee or beer. She never asked him where he'd been. The scent of companionship was on him. He stopped wanting Pamela. She was just as happy. But occasionally he came to bed with the lonely smell of cold on his skin. Those nights Pamela made love to him. Hard fast sex full of bites and scratches, raw lips and bruises. Those were the nights she wanted to leave her mark on him.

"Pamela," he'd moan. "Pamela, Pamela, Pamela." He'd come in violent spasms deep inside her. Wave after wave.

"Let's go to Niagara Falls," Pamela said one night after they'd finished. Brian's hair smelled of snow and wind. Pamela sniffed it.

Brian didn't say yes or no.

¤

Pamela did all the research, booked the hotels, checked the maps. Brian was busy at work. A new contract. He couldn't possibly get away until spring. May. That's what he said. That's what he told Pamela and Martin.

"Gotta get the show on the road," he'd say every morning as he kissed Pamela goodbye.

"'Bye, Sport," he'd say as he ruffled Martin's hair.

New staff to hire, supper with clients, late nights developing strategy. It was so clichéd Pamela is still embarrassed for not having been more suspicious. Instead of walking at night now he was working. Or so he said. He'd tiptoe into the bedroom, kiss her, then fall immediately asleep. By April, when spring came with its thaws and thickening buds and hints of warmth, Pamela had returned to her sexual self and everything seemed to be as it had been. Better, for their sex had become kinder. More light-hearted. Sweetly orgasmic.

Pamela read somewhere that good sex is normal during affairs. Another cliché. The deceiver is so turned on, so aroused, that sex is good with whomever, even the deceived. Especially the deceived. Guilt makes the deceiver anxious to please. Happiness makes anything seem possible.

¤

"It just happened," Brian said as he and Pamela stood in the front hallway. "It's not about sex. We started out talking. About you. About us. The sex took us by surprise."

"The sex is never the surprise," Pamela yelled as she kicked the suitcase until it popped open.

"This is the surprise." She walked to the front door and started slamming it over and over.

"You cancel the hotels. You tell Martin what a shit you are," she screamed and threw Brian's clothes out of the suitcase onto the floor. She couldn't stand to have his things touch hers.

"I'm not telling him for you," she screamed at his back as he walked out the door.

"Fucker!" And she ripped one of his shirts with her teeth and threw it after him.

Pamela realized he could have told her while they were in Niagara Falls. In the honeymoon suite. Instead he'd waited until they were about to leave.

"I can't go, " he'd said to her.

"Why?" she'd asked him.

"I've been seeing Suzi," he'd said. Pamela understood immediately.

"Seeing her? Or fucking her?" she'd asked.

"Both," Brian had said.

ɞ

Pamela has been sitting on the balcony off her bedroom since 3 a.m. Now it's dawn and she should go inside. Martin will be getting up for school. She doesn't want him to see her out here. To worry about her. Lately he's been spending all his free time in his room. No friends coming over, no phone calls. He listens to music, shrill, pounding music: Metallica. Aerosmith. It reminds her of Led Zeppelin and how she and her first lover, Ricky, would get stoned on hash and play "Whole Lotta Love" over and over. Ricky would lie on the floor, his head between the speakers. "Boom, bu-boom, bu-boom, bu-boompa-boom. Boom, bu-boom, bu-boom, bu-boompa-boom…Wanna whole lotta love…" Asking Pamela to move the arm of the record player back to the beginning every time the song finished.

Ricky ended up in jail. Pamela ended up hating Led Zeppelin. Whenever she asks Martin if he's OK, he says, "Yes. Don't worry. You worry too much."

She is worried, a vague shifting in her stomach, an instinct that tells her to pay attention. But she's so tired these days. Working nights. And today there is this pathetic marker of one year as an ex-wife.

The morning birds are cacophonous: red-winged black-birds, cardinals, song sparrows. And crows, of course. They make her think about her mother. Right after her sister died, her mother had come to stay. For a week. At least she said she was staying for a week. Cecily's death the geniture of her grief, Pamela's mother had moved in for five months. Pamela's father seemed to accept the change (Brian was tolerant, Martin thrilled) and came to supper every night, leaving around 8 p.m.—after pie and several cups of coffee—for home and his La-Z-Boy recliner. He wouldn't sleep in their bed alone.

"I'll be gaw-damned if I know what to do," Donny said two weeks after his wife had moved in with his daughter.

None of them knew what to do. So they fed crows. Her mother started it. First Miss Caw.

"Mumma, do you have to call it that?" Pamela asked one morning as her mother and Martin stood on the deck with bowls of food, shrieking, "Miss Caw, Miss Caw," in piercing crow-like disharmony.

"She," her mother said. "She, not it." Then she turned her back on Pamela.

"How do you know?"

"I just know," her mother said, her back still turned.

Later Miss Caw's family joined her. For hot dogs and frozen corn niblets. That's what her mother fed them.

Once, while Pamela was on her morning walk, she watched as a crow pecked the eye out of a freshly run-over squirrel.

"Miss Caw?" Pamela said to the crow, but not too loudly.

The crow had looked at her, tilted its head sideways, then continued to peck at the eyeball.

"Miss Caw would never do that," her mother said when Pamela told her what she'd seen.

"One crow, sorrow," Pamela said.

"Two crows, joy," her mother snapped.

Miss Caw liked only all-beef hotdogs. When Pamela's mother tried to feed her, at Pamela's insistence, with cheaper chicken-dogs, the crow let out a disappointed cry and cawed for over an hour, until Brian, sent to the store for the appropriate wieners, returned.

"She's nuts," Brian said.

"The crow or my mother?" Pamela asked.

A week after her mother left to go home, Pamela started having sex with Brian again.

¤

Pamela throws off her blanket and sits absorbing the early morning sun. It's been a dry spring, with record lows followed by record highs. It rained once in April and that was just a shower. Now it's May and the grass is still brown; the trees have been slow to bud. Oak trees in particular have only the tiniest of pale leaves. Some trees began to leaf, then the leaf buds died.

There's a soft munching click-click coming from the lattice on the balcony. It sounds like birds eating sunflower seeds. Or carpenter ants, which once infested the porch joists at the house Pamela and Brian sold when they divorced.

A stream of large black ants had appeared on the porch floor, hundreds of them, marching endlessly back and forth all day. Pamela and Brian and Martin had stomped on as many as they could, until they were revolted by the crunching sound of the ants' bodies and by the accumulating shiny black debris. Then at nightfall the ants disappeared.

Murdering the teeming ants so disgusted and amused them that Pamela and Brian couldn't sleep. Brian found one of his father's mildewy encyclopedias, which they'd stored in the basement for Martin. They looked up ANTS: "Camponotus (Carpenter ants). They nest in wood, invading timbers, and chewing out extensive intercommunicating chambers, which cause the wood to collapse. Unlike termites, they do not eat the wood."

They brought snacks to bed to eat while they read, drank straight scotch, re-lived their little drama. They ended up pretty drunk, and started laughing at how they must have looked out on the porch, shouting, stomping on ants. They made love.

The next morning they couldn't see any live ants, but they heard a distinct, though faint, clicking noise coming from under the porch floor. They called an exterminator. The porch was taken apart, the infested joists removed and taken to the dump, poison placed around the edges of the porch and on the floor inside the mud room. Pamela sent Martin to stay with Suzi for four days until the poison could be vacuumed up. It was like a holiday. They made love every night.

¤

Pamela checks the lattice to see if she can find the source of the noise. There is a wasp, a yellow-jacket, slowly denuding a line of greyed cedar revealing fresh pink wood underneath. The wasp flies to the roof of the balcony. Pamela watches. It's building a nest, parchment thin, grey and papery. The size of a golf ball. Pamela remembers, from helping Martin with one of his school projects, when he was obsessed by insects and started a business called Bug Busters, that the wasp will be a fertile queen.

The queen will finish building her nest, lay eggs, feed the larvae with pre-chewed insects. Some of the larvae will become queens. And some will become males, which will mate with the old queen, who will lay more eggs. The males will also fertilize the new queens. In the fall the males and old queen will die. The fertilized queens will hibernate until spring. Those that survive will start a new nest, chewing old wood from lattices and turning it into paper houses with their saliva.

Suzi and Brian have a new house. A condo on Queen Street near Victoria Park. And a new baby. All in the year since the divorce. Suzi is forty-five. Too old for babies. Pamela hopes Suzi's baby never sleeps. Ever. Martin didn't sleep through the night until just before he turned three. And during the six months before his third birthday was the first time Pamela stopped having sex with Brian. Exhaustion, pure and simple.

¤

"You go," Pamela whispered, trying to nudge Brian awake.

He seemed to mumble, but didn't wake up. Pamela was beginning to think he put this sound-sleeping act on. But she was already lifting the covers to go to Martin, whose thin frightened voice carried down the hall.

In the morning Brian would ask Pamela how many times Martin had been awake. She'd tell him.

"Wake me up, Pamela," he said.

"I try," she told him.

"How can we make this stop? Maybe we shouldn't coddle him."

When Brian said "we," Pamela slammed her coffee cup onto the table and stood up. She couldn't bear to hear Brian say "we." There was no "we" in the night.

Brian didn't hear Martin; he slept like the dead.

"Nirvana," he called his ability to fall completely asleep and hardly budge the entire night. "He must be your kid, Pamela. He can't be mine. If he was my kid he'd have no trouble sleeping the night."

It was supposed to be a joke. It wasn't funny.

"If you want sex ever again, you'll have to try to stop it," she said.

That's when Brian came up with ghost spray. To help Martin sleep alone. To let Pamela sleep the night. To help them regain their sex life. A bottle of ghost spray became a fixture on the counter in the bathroom. There were two going at all times, one for Martin, one ready when the first was emptied. The recipe: one part White Shoulders to ten parts water.

¤

White Shoulders was her mother's scent. Pamela never wore perfume. Martin loved his grandmother, with whom he shared dark, almost black hair, thick black eyelashes and a love of all living things. Except ghosts.

"Ghosts come when it's dark," Martin told them.

"You have a night light," they told him.

"But it's dark outside," Martin wailed.

Brian told him if he thought there was a ghost in his room, or under the bed, he should spray the ghost spray. It was magic. It would make the ghosts visible. Ghosts hated to be seen and they'd run away.

"Ghosts can't run," Martin corrected him. "They float."

"That's right. I forgot," Brian had said as he handed him his very first bottle of spray.

¤

Pamela was beginning to wish they'd never told Martin the lie. They thought he'd sleep knowing he was safe and in control.

"This is it, Martin. I've got to get some sleep. Where's Woo-Woo?" she asked as she handed him a fresh bottle of ghost spray.

Woo-Woo was Martin's stuffed dog, a mangy bit of worn fake fur, eyes missing, embroidered mouth shredded, a button nose replaced so many times Pamela had little cloth left to sew it to. The beloved animal smelled of stale dry bread, sweet and about to turn to mold. And a slight pissy scent. Pamela wasn't allowed to wash him. She wished he'd disintegrate so she could trash him.

Martin pulled the dog from inside his pyjama bottoms. That explained the pissy smell, Pamela thought.

"Here he is."

Martin took the ghost spray bottle and tucked it and Woo-Woo under his arm.

"'Night, Martin."

There was no answer, but as Pamela walked back to her bedroom she heard phwoosh-phwoosh. The sweet scent of White Shoulders followed her down the hall.

¤

This was the story of the night when sex returned to Pamela and Brian. The story as Pamela reconstructed it so she could tell it to Martin, who wanted to hear it over and over as he grew up.

Martin was almost three years old. At about 2 a.m., he slipped out of bed. He went to the front door, moved a chair beside it, twisted the deadbolt and slipped off the security chain. He climbed from the chair, put on his sweatshirt and his rubber boots. He went outside. It was drizzling. He had Woo-Woo and the fresh bottle of ghost spray with him. He started down the street.

He walked about four blocks before Peter Wilkins, a security guard driving home from a split shift, spotted Martin walking alone. Martin was crying. Peter Wilkins stopped and asked Martin if he was lost.

"No," Martin said.

Peter suggested that Martin go home, but Martin said he wanted to go to Gary's house. Gary had a Batman night-light. Peter asked if he knew where Gary lived.

"Yes," Martin said.

"I'll follow you to make sure you get there," Peter told Martin.

He didn't want to frighten Martin by taking him in his car. He parked and followed Martin, talking to him quietly about the weather and the stuffed dog Martin had locked under his arm.

Martin walked to Gary's. He knocked on the door. After a while Suzi answered. Peter made sure Martin knew Suzi and Suzi knew Martin, left his phone number and address, and went home. When Pamela called him the next morning to thank him for helping Martin, he asked about the spray bottle. Pamela explained about the ghost spray. He laughed. He told her that Martin kept falling as he walked. Tripping. He had his boots on the wrong feet and his kangaroo jacket on upside down, the wet hood dragging between his legs.

"I didn't want to scare him, so I didn't touch him even though I wanted to pick him up and carry him wherever it was he wanted to go."

Martin's spray bottle was empty, Peter said.

When Suzi brought Martin home, Brian thanked her. Pamela hugged Martin, then hugged Suzi, and cried.

"Bed now," Brian said to Martin and took him by the hand, led him away.

Pamela didn't tell Martin this part of the story. The night after Martin's adventure he slept and slept and slept. That midnight Pamela found herself awake and wandering the house, waiting for Martin to need more ghost spray. He didn't. Around five she crawled back into bed with Brian and pinched the pale soft underside his arm as hard as she could until he woke up.

"Shit, Pamela, what are you doing?" Brian lifted his arm to look at the spot she'd been pinching.

"Let's fuck," she said.

The bruise on Brian's arm lasted three weeks.

Pamela folds her blanket and brings it into her bedroom. She left work early, something she never does. She said she was feeling sick. But really she was distracted and found she was making mistakes. Not a good thing to do when you're dealing with money. She'd taken the job at the armoured car company two months after Brian left. She'd been the part-time assistant manager at a bookstore, but she only made a little more than minimum wage. When she asked for more money and more hours, the storeowner said no.

She sent out one hundred and seven résumés and had two interviews, one for a job where they told her they already had a candidate in mind but thought they should finish the interview process just in case. The second interview went well, but she never received a call. When she called to see if a decision had been made, the receptionist said she'd have the manager phone Pamela. No one phoned.

When she applied for the armoured car company job, two hundred and ten other people also applied. There was a write-up about it in the newspaper: "Recession," the headline screamed. There was a photo of part of the line-up. Pamela was in the photo wearing her brown dress pants and white shirt, a jacket over her shoulder. She hated that Brian and Suzi would see the picture. Martin loved it. He cut it out and pinned it to their bulletin board. Pamela was one of twelve who were hired.

She works nights. It isn't the best situation, but she is home in the morning when Martin gets ready for school and she gets out of bed at 3:30 p.m., so she is around when he gets home. He is supposed to be in bed before she leaves for work at eleven, but sometimes he's still awake. He can call Brian if he has any problems, and twice a week her mother comes for supper and falls asleep on the couch watching TV, then wakes up for breakfast when Pamela gets home. Her father, who also works shifts, joins them. They eat bacon and eggs and hash browns with ketchup and lots of toast dripping butter and rhubarb ginger jam. Sometimes Pamela has a beer.

"How can you do that?" her mother asks.

"It's her supper," Pamela's father says. "Lots of people come home after work and have a beer with their supper."

Pamela had to pass three separate psychological tests with questions like: Do you get nervous in confined spaces? Would you consider taking paper clips from your workplace a theft; do you consider yourself an honest person? Do you now, or have you ever, smoked marijuana?

There was also a physical with a urine test for drugs for which she had to sign a permission form. There was an application for a Firearms Acquisition Certificate and a gun Permit to Carry. There was computer training. She had to be fingerprinted at the police station. There was shooting practice on the firing range, and final testing. Pamela passed everything. She was number one, her supervisor told her, the top of her group.

This morning, when she went to her supervisor to ask if she minded if Pamela left early, her supervisor asked if she had a minute.

"Pigs and cowboys," her supervisor said. "The guys here, it's all guns and dicks. Barry from Armoured told me he was sleeping with Darlene from the Money Room. 'So why are you telling me?' I asked him. He says, 'Why not? All the guys sleep with Darlene. They hate her guts, but they sleep with her anyway.' I asked him why. 'Because she lets them blow their wad,' he said. Now what do I say to that?"

"I don't know," Pamela said. "I'll be in tomorrow night for sure."

Darlene is twenty-six. She has weary grey eyes, thick auburn hair, freckled happy-looking skin. She works part-time and has two other part-time jobs as well. "Have to pay the rent," she told Pamela. As soon as she's made full-time in one job, she'll quit the others. In her free time she drifts from one man to another, debris caught in a current, snagging here or there. Random, temporary docking.

Pamela had slept with a hard-body from work, too. For a month or so. Rob Hastings. He had arms as thick as her waist, a chest with more muscles than seemed possible. Some of them danced, rhythmic jumping, when he wanted them to. The sex hadn't been particularly good, which surprised though didn't disappoint Pamela. She knew the affair was a mistake before she even started, and because the sex wasn't good it had been easier to give it up.

Rob liked guns and motorcycles and money, though he only made a bit more an hour than she did, which wasn't much. He was smart and sweet. He had very little imagination, liked to be on top every time. No variation. But Pamela loved the feel of him on her, his weight a pleasure to bear. Significant. He wasn't angry when she told him she wouldn't sleep with him anymore. They remained civil, even friendly. He didn't want it known that he had slept with a woman twenty years his senior.

Pamela still likes to touch the silky oiled softness of the skin that sheathes his hard arm muscles. He lets her, but it's all play, nothing more than goes on with the other women on the shift. "Wanna feel my muscle?" he says and thrusts his hips forward. Then he pulls up his sleeve and flexes his bicep. "Ah," the women in the Money Room say as they feel his muscle.

And Pamela likes Darlene. Her energy, her ready smile, the way her fingers move so quickly over the keys of her computer.

✠

Suzi came to see Pamela yesterday. Pamela didn't let her in, made her stand at the door. "I'm Martin's stepmother. Shouldn't we begin to talk, for the kids' sakes, for Martin and Gary, and the new baby, Jess?" Suzi said. She wanted to know if they could ever be friends again, if Pamela could ever forgive her. She missed Pamela, she said, they'd been so close for so many years.

Suzi was tall, and terribly thin for someone who'd just had a baby. Pamela had sometimes worried that Suzi was bulimic, had asked her about it once, but Suzi just laughed. She ate more food than anyone Pamela knew, man or woman.

She had a broad open smile, wonderful white teeth, large honest eyes and a thrilled astonished laugh, as though humour always took her by surprise. Her hands were graceful, and she had a shiny new wedding ring that slid up and down her fine-boned finger. She wore a button-down collar oxford cloth shirt, pale pink. Pressed blue jeans. Topsiders. She didn't look like a slut.

Pamela stood with her arms crossed, listening. Looking over Suzi's shoulder. Listening and listening. When Suzi stopped talking she stood some more.

"Pamela?"

Pamela turned, went inside, and very quietly, very gently, closed the door.

¤

"Mom!"

Pamela turns from the balcony railing and goes into her bedroom.

"I'm in my room," she calls.

Martin's hair is long; he started growing it in the fall. It is dark and glossy, thick and tangled, and droops over his eyes. He plunks down on her bed.

"Grandma called last night and said to tell you she and Grandpa are coming to supper tonight. They'll pick up some Kentucky Fried."

"What time?"

"Five-thirty. They want to have a visit. You'll be up by then?"

"Yup."

Pamela wants to push Martin's hair from his eyes.

"You better get going," she says. "You'll be late."

Martin gets up and walks to the door. He turns.

"Grandma said to be nice to you. She said it'll be a hard day." Martin looks so serious, so sad. He shrugs his shoulders and leaves.

Pamela sees Brian in that shrug, in those shoulders. She sees lots of Brian in Martin, but tries to see only the good parts. Martin had lived a week on, a week off with his father for three months before he asked Brian if he could live with Pamela full time instead of splitting his time between households. Brian was gracious. Martin lives with Pamela and spends every other weekend with Brian and Suzi, Gary and baby Jess.

Once, soon after the separation, when Pamela and Martin had moved, and Pamela was still raw and filled with anger, when she refused to talk to Brian, refused to have anything to do with him and used Martin, unfairly, as a go-between, Martin asked her if she had ever loved his father because she seemed to hate him so much now.

"Of course I did," she told Martin, but she wondered if that was true because at that time she couldn't remember loving him, couldn't think of why she would have. Lately she sometimes does remember, in alarming detail, like the day Brian proposed.

They had been living together for a year and were on holiday in Nova Scotia, spending the afternoon at Lawrencetown Beach. The water was cool, but the day was bright and hot, the sky endless, the ocean too. They were packing the car to go back to their rented cabin. Pamela was leaning into the trunk arranging lawn chairs, towels, their picnic basket, the thermos. When she stood up, Brian was gone. She scanned the dunes, then the beach, then the water. She saw him.

Brian was swimming toward a child floating in an inner tube. The child's skin looked pale and too soft against the shiny hard blackness of the rubber. The tube was caught on the current and was drifting out to sea. Drifting further and further away.

Pamela went to the water's edge. She was alone. No one noticed the child. The wind off the shore slivered bits of sand into the backs of her bare legs. It carried fragments of sound: gulls' screams, the squeals of children, the rumble of a truck along the road. Pamela was sure Brian was talking to the child, sure he was reassuring him that everything would be fine, just fine. She was sure she could see his lips moving, though that was impossible.

When Brian had nearly reached the child, he tossed a rope. Pamela couldn't remember there being a rope in the car, or when Brian might have taken it. He threw it three...four...five times.

The child finally grabbed the rope. Brian turned and swam toward the beach. Pamela noticed the scent of rotting fish, of brine, and of the coconut of suntan lotion. She noticed the glisten of sun on the backs of glassy waves, a woman bobbing on the rise and fall of swells, her huge breasts like cabbages in her faded green bathing suit.

It was then that people noticed what was happening. Several men waded into the shallows, then stopped. No one swam out into the water. A large woman in a black bathing suit ran to the shore, called, "Perry! Perry!" Over and over, as though by calling he would come.

When Brian could stand, he turned and pulled the rope toward him. He grabbed the inner tube and pulled it, and the child, closer. The child's bathing suit was two toned, red and blue. Two men, one with a minuscule yellow bathing suit slung low beneath his grand hairy belly, waded out to help. The woman ran into the water, droplets sparkling, shooting from her heels. She hauled the child off the tube.

"What were you doing?" she cried, hugging the child to her. "Whatever did you think you were doing?"

A crowd had gathered to watch. Brian walked toward Pamela coiling the rope as he came.

"Brian," she said.

He brushed her arm, his skin cold and salt-sticky. He walked past her. She turned and followed. He put the rope in the car, took a towel and rubbed his hair, under his arms, his groin and legs. She took the towel from him and rubbed his back, handed him the dry shirt she somehow happened to have over her arm. He opened the car door and sat on the edge of the frame. He started to shiver. Pamela told him to stand up. He did. She took him in her arms and began to rub his body. All over. As hard as she could. She could hear his teeth chattering.

As the shivering lessened, Brian began to sob. She turned him, made him sit in the passenger seat. She closed the door and went to the driver's side. As she started the car she saw that the crowd still stood at the edge of the water. The mother and child were nowhere to be seen. The black inner tube bobbed over rushing waves, up, down. Up. Down. Pamela started the car and they drove back to the cabin.

Brian stripped. He crawled into bed naked, still crying. He asked her to come and lie beside him and she did. He cried until he fell asleep. Pamela got out of bed. She dressed and sat beside him. She watched him sleep. It was the first night they had not made love since they started living together a year before.

Brian awoke near dawn. He asked her if she would marry him.

¤

After Martin leaves for school, Pamela runs a bath. She pours a glass of brandy and lies back in the water. She dozes and awakens, sips her drink. She should go to bed soon or she'll be overtired and won't sleep well in the afternoon. But for now she is content. One year as an ex-wife. An anniversary. Kentucky Fried Chicken to mark the occasion. She hears the birds through the open window, the traffic, a group of girls laughing as they walk to school.

¤

Before Suzi divorced Philip, just after she first separated from him, but not before she'd first slept with Brian, though Pamela didn't know that yet, Pamela went with her to Toronto. For a break. Suzi seemed unbearably sad and even thinner than usual.

Pamela visited the ROM, spent hours looking at Egyptian mummies. She visited the art gallery and sat in coffee bars in Yorkville reading expensive glossy magazines. She took the ferry to Toronto Island, walked, smiled at passing cyclists.

While Pamela played tourist, Suzi visited a man, a real estate broker she had dated when she was young. She visited him at his home where he and his wife lived. She played with their young son. Sometimes Suzi met the man in an office he was showing. They made love on the carpet. They left the lights on. There were no curtains on the windows.

Late at night, in the hotel room she shared with Pamela, Suzi said she didn't care who saw them making love through the curtainless windows. Suzi cried and told Pamela about her marriage. About how suspicious Philip had been. He thought she was having an affair. That's why they had separated. She wasn't really having an affair; the real estate broker was a one-time deal. But Philip had thought her tears, her distance, her extreme thinness, the fact that she was away from home so often for work, meant she was seeing someone else.

Pamela was Suzi's friend. She listened to Suzi tell her about the real estate broker. About his wife. About the room they made love in. She listened to Suzi tell her about her bad marriage and how lucky Pamela was to have Brian. He was so strong, so sure of himself. So honest and caring.

Pamela listened and listened. She didn't want Suzi to be so hurt. She wanted to be Suzi's friend forever. She didn't tell Suzi about the man she'd just met at the restaurant who sat with her every afternoon for coffee. They talked and talked. She didn't tell her how she had invited him up to the room she shared with Suzi one afternoon. How they had undressed each other slowly and tentatively, the curtains drawn, the lights dimmed. She didn't mention that before they had even made love she'd asked the man to stop touching her. She had turned away from him and locked herself in the bathroom. When she came out, after bathing and washing her hair, he was gone.

Pamela listened to Suzi. Maybe she felt a little smug. But she didn't want Suzi to be so hurt, so she listened and listened. She never, ever, said a word.

Night Watch

There's a courteous anarchy to night driving. The rules exist: stop signs, traffic lights, lines on the road. Drivers acknowledge them, pause at red lights before breezing through, put their flashers on when they drive the wrong way on the wrong side of the street (these mostly oil truck drivers, emergency repairmen and newspaper deliverers). Everyone speeds, including Pamela.

Night cars are big. Vans with logos on their sides, Cadillacs, Lincoln Continentals, taxis, dump trucks and big old Chevys with rust and rolled-down windows, blue-black exhaust billowing in all directions. Big cars could be going anywhere. Small cars are going home, or in the direction of hospitals; otherwise, like children, they shouldn't be out.

Pamela's a tidy five-four, average weight. She's long-waisted and, at forty-eight, still has a twenty-four inch belt size, which is just as well, she likes to joke, because she has no breasts to speak of. Her small waist gives the impression of there being a chest above it.

She's efficient, her movements quick and spare. She does her job and she does it well. If there are any complaints she doesn't take them personally. No big deal. Pamela just wishes that being Martin's mother was half as easy.

She swings her car onto Lancaster Street. Soft tires squeal on hot asphalt. Feverish air pounds in through the window, whips Pamela's hair across her face and into her mouth.

This night is sultry, the sky starry but blurred at the edges. The air blowing in her car window smells of heated asphalt, and a hint of rain. Pamela is on her way to the armoured car security company where she's been working night shifts for the last three years. Since her divorce from Brian.

Sometimes she works straight nights—twelve to eight. Lately she's been working a bridging shift from four until noon. Counting money, which every night sifts from bags to counters, and back into the bags Pamela labels with destinations: Bank of Canada. External Affairs. Eaton's. Millions of dollars.

Pamela doesn't have millions of dollars. Her car is a rusty old grey Chevy Impala. The side door and the trunk won't open; the front right tire refuses to hold air for more than ten days. The passenger mirror is held on with duct tape. Oil leaks onto her driveway. The radio throws static no matter where she places the dial.

Pamela feels an unbounded affection for this car. It makes her feel secure. That she can afford to run it gives her a sense of freedom: she could get in and go anywhere: St.-Louis-du-Ha! Ha! or Regina. Vancouver or Washington, D.C. It's the one thing she owns she doesn't share with Martin, even though he's had his licence for over a year now. He can drive Brian and Suzi's car, but when he's with her, he walks, or takes the bus, or has Pamela pick him up.

Martin's almost nineteen. He's as handsome as a movie star and could charm the panties off a nun. He has brown, almost black eyes which he lines with kohl, lush dark lashes. He's dyed his curly raven-black hair blond and cut it to within an inch of his scalp. He smokes cigarettes (but not in the house) and marijuana (but not in the house), has developed a taste for micro-brewery beer (fewer chemicals, he says) and a distaste for school. He has a girlfriend named Janey. "I'd marry her," he told Pamela, "if I was older, but I'm not."

Martin wrote an essay in the eleventh grade, a year after the divorce, in which he intimated he'd been close to suicide, been confused and depressed. He left it on the dining room table and when Pamela read it she cried, then asked him if he wanted to see a doctor; if they should get some help. Martin told her that the depression had passed; it was when he was younger, in grade nine. He just said it was that year in the essay.

He bent down and hugged her (he was six foot-one) and kissed her on the forehead, which also made her cry. He said, "I'm fine. Don't worry, Mom. You're always worrying."

Martin was arrested for possession of narcotics (marijuana) when he was seventeen. Pamela learned later that the police took the handcuffs off just before they brought him to the front door. (Handcuffs on Martin, Pamela thought, when Martin told her this part of the story.) Two policemen handed Martin over to Pamela as she stood in the cold of the open door in her flannelette nightie. (These cops look like babies, and this nightie is coming part at the seams, she noticed.) Martin wasn't even stopped for drugs, he told her after the police had left, but because he didn't have his seatbelt done up. (I'll have to ground him for the seatbelt, she told herself.) When he rolled down the car window the smell of the joint he'd been smoking drifted into the young policeman's face.

Martin got an absolute discharge. Pamela spent days in court, days she should have been sleeping because she had to work at night. She sat with terrified parents and some frightened children.

Other children were cocky, defiant. "Fuck you, cunt," one sweet-faced boy said when she asked him to please move his splayed legs to let her get past. These most often came to court alone. Pamela could only suppose their parents had given up on them. One child didn't turn up for his court appearance and a warrant was put out for his arrest. ("My God, Martin," Pamela whispered, "a warrant.")

Martin was one of the frightened ones, grateful to have her there, a bit smart-assy when it was over. They didn't even get the seatbelt fine, he said, as he bent over to undo his shiny black bought-for-court lace-ups and changed into the running shoes he'd asked Pamela to bring with her in her knapsack.

Pamela told him she thought it would be best for him to shut up. She told him to put some of his smart thinking into how they were going to pay the lawyer on her twelve-dollar-an-hour wage. She reminded Martin that his father thought he should be paying his own legal fees.

Sometimes, when Pamela's driving to work at night, she compares her childhood to Martin's. Hers had been filled with early responsibility. With no expectation beyond getting out, getting a job, and being able to look after herself. And marriage, of course. There was always marriage.

Martin's childhood had been middle-class and comfortable until the divorce: lessons, birthday parties, friends in every day after school. Vacations to Florida, Cape Breton, beaches on Lake Huron. Even after the divorce, Brian gave Martin an allowance and offered to pay for university courses Pamela could never afford. Courses Martin now disdained.

As Pamela turns onto Lancaster Street, a luminous thin slice of moon hangs before her in the velvety blue-black sky. Orion—her favourite constellation, because she can always find it—gleams above her. Pamela remembers a summer of tent building and nights of sleeping out, nights with skies like this one. She and Cecily and their friends gathered blankets, old tablecloths, tarps—anything cloth—and fastened them to the fence with clothespins, then strung them over the clothesline. Rooms were fashioned. Pillows, bedding, bags of cherries and potato chips, flashlights, pyjamas (no boys, never any boys), bottles of pop, warm and too fizzy by the time they were opened, were gathered and set up.

Most of the fun was in the set-up. Once night came, someone, Cecily maybe, never Pamela, would go inside to pee, or worse, poop, because that couldn't be done on the lawn. Another would start to wheeze because one of the blankets had been slept on by the dog and they were allergic. The tents were too hot and airless, no windows having been made, so they'd take a blanket and lie on the grass, gazing at the sky trying to keep their eyes from closing, listening to night sounds, to the sound that would send them scurrying back into the tent.

By morning Pamela and Cecily would be alone, their
friends having wandered home throughout the night. They'd be
cranky, tired and sweaty, and have stomach aches from too many
cherries and too much warm pop. Pamela's mother swore,
"Never again," but she always forgot, happy to have her daughters out of her hair for a while. Happy for a moment's peace.

Martin had never made a tent to sleep in outdoors. He'd
been to camp, to cottages, had stayed in motels and hotels.
Maybe that's what's missing for Martin, Pamela thinks, spending long summer afternoons building blanket tents, sleeping in
them under starry skies, getting too hot, getting stomach cramps.

A pretty weak theory, Pamela thinks. They all are. But this
is her routine. As she drives to work at night, she thinks about
what could—or should—have happened to Martin that might have
prevented him from going at life head-on. Compares his life to hers.

And it comes down to this: Pamela remembers her childhood, remembers boyfriends who were too fast and driving in
cars with drunk people at the wheel. She remembers smoking
dope and never getting caught. She remembers all this and she
knows none of it, not one bit, has anything to do with Martin.

This morning, when Pamela got up at 3 a.m., she heard
music coming from Martin's room. She ran up to turn it off
thinking he'd left it on before he went out. (Some nights Pamela
passes Martin on the stairs. He's coming in; she's leaving for
work. "You can't keep this up," she tells him. Martin watches
her, eyes dreamy, heavy-lidded. "'Night, Mom," is all he says.)

She opened his door and was about to enter when she saw,
illuminated in the moonlight coming through the window, the
pale, almost translucent naked body of Janey lying on top of the
muscular naked body of Martin. Pamela was apologetic, backed
out of the room as quickly as possible. Thinking, they're so
beautiful. Thinking, am I ready for what this means? Thinking,
Janey has socks on, big red woollen ones.

Pamela parks her car. The air remains hot but now smells
of cut grass and diesel oil. The night sky's cleared, become
brilliant, lovely, the horn of the waning moon crowned by

glowing Venus. So lovely it makes tears come to her eyes. This moon is the same one that shone on Janey's perfect skin.

Pamela's buzzed into the building by the tower guard and again through to the gun lockers where she loads her revolver. The signs on the wall read, "Confidence in your gun handling ability can mark you as a fellow-employee whom others will welcome on the job and on the range." And, "The old saying that familiarity breeds contempt does not apply to guns." Pamela's always nervous when she must qualify in her semi-annual shoot, but she passes, firing all her rounds straight into the heart of the torso-shaped target.

Even though Martin claims to be a pacifist, that Pamela can shoot a gun impresses him. "My mom," Martin says, then smiles and pats her on the shoulder.

"You don't want to end up like me," Pamela once shouted at Martin during a fight about school, about missing classes and getting low marks.

"No fear," Martin laughed. "I'll never work nights because then I wouldn't be able to party."

"Martin!" Pamela cried.

"You're too serious," Martin sighed, and he turned and walked away from her.

¤

Pamela buys a pop from the machine and is buzzed into the Money Room, the bleak, windowless concrete bunker where she will spend the next eight hours. She notices immediately that the familiar constant whirr of the counting machines is absent. All the work stations are closed. Everyone's standing—quiet and unmoving—in the break room, except for two men who are standing beside Pamela's work station in the far corner of the counting room.

Jack, a baby-faced twenty-five-year-old ex-hockey player, who's six-two and built like a sumo wrestler, towers over Francis. Francis is sixty-three, diabetic thin, his grey hair slicked into an Elvis burlesque. His joints are deteriorating due to arthritis; his fingers are a rubbery twisted parody of what fingers should be.

In his former life Francis had been a bank manager who found the stress, and the occasion to drink at luncheons, too debilitating. Often he has gout.

"Fuck you, fuck you, old man," Jack screams, and his body mass seems to expand further, rises up and suspends itself above Francis. His meaty red fists clench and unclench at his side. Sweat beads across his upper lip, circles under his armpits.

Francis's neck and ears glow. Neon. He shoves his face right up into Jack's. He presses his lips into a thin tight line over his teeth, and makes a sound like a hiss, but he doesn't say a word.

Both men are wearing loaded guns, Smith & Wesson .38 calibre police and military revolvers. Each has six extra bullets in the speed loader attached to his gun belt.

"You're finished, old man." Spit sprays onto Francis as Jack shouts.

Pamela's like a donkey with the bulls. Her gender and age command respect; her efficient let's-get-this-show-on-the-road attitude soothes. Jack and Francis have been feuding for weeks. As Pamela moves toward them, the men turn her way and immediately the tension diffuses. And before she even speaks, Pamela's thinking how she will relate this story to Martin, the words she'll use to make him laugh, but also to make him hear, Stay in school.

Later Pamela's supervisor tells her that Jack's just started to take Prozac for depression, and to calm his temper. Francis is going on a leave of absence and will enter a treatment centre. "That should help," she says.

¤

It's one-thirty in the afternoon, a humid thirty-six degrees, when Pamela gets home from work. Martin's unwashed breakfast dishes sit on the counter. Martin is, she hopes, at school; this is his last week before exams. She undresses, showers, and pulls down the blinds. When Pamela first started nights and had to learn how to sleep in daylight she wore a sleeping mask. It made her and Martin laugh, but it did the trick. Now she sleeps without it, in fact has no trouble sleeping anytime, day or night.

She also turns on the air conditioner, her one indulgence since the divorce.

Pamela has Friday off. At her suggestion, she and Martin are going out to lunch, doing some shopping, meeting Janey, then going to a movie, all of this a concession to her because she sees so little of Martin and it matters to her that she doesn't. Pamela arranged the day off weeks before, but it will be classified as a sick day so she can be paid and still have all her holidays. She never takes sick days, always forges on when she gets ill, takes aspirin, decongestant, antibiotics, whatever it takes. She knows this is obsessive behaviour but she can't help it.

Perhaps that's where Martin gets his obsessions. He's always had one following another as he grew up: Transformers, Lego, G.I. Joe, snakes, setting up businesses—Pet Finders Inc., Bug Busters Inc.—and then guitars and music. He read every book he could get hold of about what he was doing, created elaborate schemes for adventure, fame, success. As he became more and more involved with marijuana and girls, and less and less with school or anything else, Pamela lamented the child she felt she'd lost. She even told Martin, asked him where he thought that child had gone. Martin had taken her hand, looked at her quietly, but never answered her question.

Later, with a sense of relief and foreboding, Pamela realized that Martin was as dedicated to marijuana as he had been to his childhood hobbies. He knew everything there was to know about it. He read magazines and books, did research projects at school (these his only As), knew how to grow it indoors and out. He knew what illnesses it was good for: nausea relief from chemotherapy, from motion sickness, from the side-effects of some medications. Appetite stimulation for anorexics, the depressed, the elderly and those with AIDS. A sedative for insomnia.

He knew the laws, mostly unfair, in his opinion. Particularly for possession, Martin said, considering the cost to taxpayers for prosecuting simple possession cases. And if it was legalized, think of all the money the government would make in taxes, he expounded. When he talked about marijuana, he was evangelistic. Crusading.

When Pamela gets up around ten, it's still hot and Martin's still not home. There aren't any messages on the machine. Usually he calls if he isn't coming home. "It's the least you can do," she yelled at him during one fight about late nights and missed meals, and he finally agreed.

These days, when Pamela worries about Martin not coming home, she thinks that soon he won't be living with her anymore. He'll be nineteen in the fall, a birthday he's already planning how to celebrate: lunch with Brian and Suzi and Gary and Jess, a special meal with Janey and Pamela, then off to the bars with a group of young men.

Several of Martin's friends already have their own apartments, two live with their girlfriends. Martin's leaving will be too soon, and exactly right, Pamela thinks, and Martin will hate it that she'll cry.

Pamela remembers when Martin was born, how she cried. Some of it for joy at his perfection, some because she was exhausted. But the real reason she never talked about, tried not to think about. She cried because his blood didn't beat with the same rhythm as hers. Right from the second the cord between them was cut he became himself. And at that moment she thought the words she could never speak, "My beautiful perfect child will die someday, and I've made this possible."

Pamela wanders into Martin's room, the sheets still tangled from his love-making with Janey. She sees his guitar, his magazines, his clothes. She picks up a shirt and sniffs it, inhaling his man-child odour, a mix of deodorant and sweat, and a sweetness like spun sugar, at once so familiar and so foreign.

She takes the shirt with her as she goes into the bathroom. The note is taped to the mirror:

> I've gone off to the circus. I'm going to drink alcohol, do drugs and have sex. I'll be back at one.
>
> Martin

Pamela drops the shirt onto the floor and pulls the note from the mirror. She folds the tape back onto the paper. She folds the paper corner to corner, and corner to corner again, into a perfect square, and creases each edge with her fingernails. The scent of warmed paper rises. She places the note in her pocket, washes her hands and face. Brushes her teeth. Combs her hair, for tonight Pamela's working at twelve-thirty. A shipment of gold is arriving and she's been asked to arrange for its transport.

At midnight she steps outside, ready for her night ride, prepared to begin her night watch. After she locks the door, Pamela uncreases Martin's note, then, standing in the magnificent pulsing heat, she reads it again by porch light. Turning away from the light, turning toward the darkness, Pamela walks to her Chevy, checks the right tire and gets in. As the engine rumbles alive, Pamela begins to laugh.

And she laughs. And laughs. And laughs.

Susan Zettell was born and raised in Kitchener, Ontario. She has also lived in Cambridge, Vancouver, Cape Breton and Halifax, and now resides in Ottawa. She is a graduate of Dalhousie and Carleton Universities. A number of the stories in *Night Watch* have been previously published in *The Fiddlehead, Pottersfield Portfolio, Canadian Forum* and *The New Quarterly*. Zettell's first collection of short stories, *Holy Days of Obligation*, was published in 1998. Her poetry, reviews and articles have also been widely published and she has stories in the recently published anthologies *Quintet, Spider Women: A Tapestry of Creativity and Healing* and *The Day the Men Went to Town*.

MEMBRE DU GROUPE SCABRINI

Québec, Canada
2000